MISSY'S MOMENT

THE WEST SERIES

JILL SANDERS

GRAYTON

To my favorite readers…
Yeah, you.

SUMMARY

Melissa is back in Fairplay, Texas for good. After taking over the small health clinic in town, she finally feels like she has everything she's ever wanted. But when Reece West walks into the clinic, she finds something she didn't even know she wanted. Now she'll do just about anything to get the man of her dreams.

Reece is looking for trouble, and he's found it at Saddleback Ranch. He can ride hard, rope some steer, and train the horses that he can finally afford. But when he bumps into little Missy Holton again, his world will turn upside down.

PROLOGUE

$\mathcal{R}$eece wiped the blood from his nose and yanked his chin up so his pa wouldn't see that the blow had damaged his soul. When his brother, Ryan, moved to help him up from the dirt, he shook his head to stop him.

"You like hitting little kids, old man?" He stood up and dusted off his Levi's like he had all the time in the world.

"Little brats who don't listen to me deserve to have their asses kicked." His old man stood almost a foot taller than Reece's thirteen-year-old frame. He couldn't wait for the day when he would be taller than the old man, because he knew that was the day he'd walk away and never look back.

"Pa, it was my fault." Ryan started to cover for him. Even though the boys were identical in looks, they were complete opposites in personality.

"I'm the one who didn't shut the gate after Pa asked," Reece said, squinting his eyes at his twin. "I'll go hunt down the horses."

His father grunted and threw him the reins to Buck, his stallion. "Be back by supper time or you won't get any slop." Reece watched his father walk away without a backward glance.

"Hang on a few minutes, and I'll saddle up Star," Ryan said before rushing towards the barn.

"No," Reece called out. "Star will just slow me down. I can get the damn horses myself." He jumped on the back of Buck and hightailed it out of the yard.

The dry heat of the day turned to a cool breeze as he flew across the yellow fields. He knew where the three horses would go first, the stream, so he headed towards it with a smile on his face.

This is what he lived for, a moment to himself as he rode across the fields. No old man slapping at you, no brother sticking up for you. Just him and a horse. He leaned down and patted Buck on the neck. "You like to run, don't you?" He smiled when the horse nodded his head. He had a way with animals; they always seemed to listen and never gave him shit back.

It took him almost two hours to get to the stream, and by the time he gathered the three horses and tied their leads together, he was covered in sweat and dirt. Tying the rope to a tree, he pulled off his soiled clothes and jumped in the cool water for a swim.

After ten minutes in the cool water, he calculated that he wouldn't get home until an hour after dark. Damn. He was hungry.

Pulling his dirty clothes on, he jumped on Buck's back and yanked the other horses to follow him. When he finally rode up, the back-porch light was the only one on in the small house. It had taken him too long to get back, mostly because he hadn't wanted to injure a horse by rushing in the dark.

There wasn't a warm plate in the oven waiting for him, no sweet note from a mother telling him to eat something—nothing. Except for an empty feeling as he climbed the dark stairs with achy muscles and a sore backside from the long ride.

When Reece sat down on his bed, Ryan sat up and flipped on the small light.

"I saved you a sandwich." He nodded to a plate sitting on the box he used as a nightstand.

"Thanks."

"Were they at the stream?"

"Yeah," he said in between bites.

"Damn, I'm sorry, man."

Reece shrugged his shoulders. "My fault."

"Man, I can't wait till the day we can get out of here." Ryan lay back down and stared up at the ceiling.

It was a common conversation of theirs. They'd been planning their escape since a month after their mother had passed of cancer shortly after their tenth birthday. That's when their dad had turned mean.

"Yeah, till then, I guess I need to make sure I close the gate."

Ryan chuckled. "Did you enjoy the ride, at least?"

Reece nodded. "Best moment of the month so far." He smiled at his brother and flipped off the light. The two boys lay on their beds, identical dreams of escaping in their heads as they drifted off.

Melissa walked into the empty clinic and smiled. The small waiting room was quiet, but she knew that within the hour, it would be full of crying kids and worrying mamas. She'd never imagined herself back in her hometown, taking over the clinic that everyone in town had been in at some moment in their lives.

"Well?" her older brother said from behind her. "What do you think?" Grant wrapped his arm around her shoulders and smiled down at her.

She smiled up at him, wanting to squeal with joy. "Thanks for buying me breakfast." She nodded to the coffee in her hand. He'd taken her to Mama's, the best—and only—diner in town. It had just been remodeled and was busier than ever.

Melissa was staying with Grant, his wife, Alex, and their daughter, Laura, out at their new ranch just outside of town. At least until she could find a place of her own.

There were a few possibilities, but she had yet to make up her mind about which one to move in to.

It had been almost two weeks since she'd returned to town and had bumped into Dr. Conner, who had quickly informed her that he was looking to hire a new head nurse for the clinic. Bonnie, the head nurse who had worked at the clinic for as long as anyone could remember, had retired earlier that year. Dr. Conner had told her that he was desperate to hire someone who could put things in order again around the clinic. He was about ten years older than Melissa and had been working at the clinic since moving into town almost six years ago. Melissa had noted that he wasn't a bad looking man; he was tall, had jet-black hair and dark eyes, something she'd always found very attractive in a man. She'd worked with plenty of doctors in Houston where she'd gone to school and done her internship, but she had immediately wondered about working with Dr. Conner since it was a small town and people talked.

She'd run into him at the grocery store, and he'd almost begged her to at least stop by and look into the clinic. She'd put it off for a while, but after applying for a few jobs in the city, she'd decided that sticking around her hometown for a while couldn't hurt.

When she had stopped by, all the other employees had been so accepting and kind, and when Dr. Conner had presented her with an offer, she'd jumped at it.

Now as she looked around the room, she couldn't help but smile.

"Anytime, little sis." He leaned down and placed a kiss on her cheek. "Anytime. Well, I'd better get back to the house. I bet my girls are up already."

She smiled, remembering how cute her niece was. Her soft blonde hair, chubby baby cheeks, and eyes matched Grant's perfectly.

"Go be a husband and daddy." She reached up and kissed his cheek. He had changed so much in the past few years that she still had a hard time believing he was the same man. Gone were the chubby cheeks, the thick glasses, and the insecurity. Now her brother looked more like a movie star than the awkward boy she'd been raised looking up to, which only made her look up to him even more.

By the time she'd flipped on all the lights in the clinic, several of the staff had arrived and were preparing for the day. Since Fairplay was a small town, she already knew everyone who worked there. When the doctor walked in at a quarter past eight, the waiting room and the three small examining rooms were already full. Apparently, it was early flu season and most of the kids in grade school had passed it to one another.

By the end of her first day, she was exhausted and yet strangely full of energy. She knew there was a lot she could improve on at the small clinic and hoped that everyone else would be as excited as she was to make things flow more efficiently. During her lunch, she had written up a small list of items she would fix first.

After the doors were closed and locked for the day, she knocked on Dr. Conner's office door.

"Come in." She took a deep breath and opened the door.

"Oh, Melissa," he said, setting down a folder. He waved her in and motioned to the chair. "So, how was your first day?"

"Great." She smiled, feeling a little nervous.

"I can't thank you enough for helping us out. So, what did you think?" He folded his arms on the desk and waited.

She took a deep breath. "I have a few suggestions." She looked down at the paper in her hands.

"Great." He held out his hand for the paper.

She waited as he read through her list, her fingers folded in her lap, and her eyes focused on his face, waiting for any emotions.

"These could all work out very well." He smiled and looked up at her. "Some of them might take some time for us to adjust to, but I think we can all make an effort. When would you like to start on these?"

Her eyebrows shot up. There was no arguing, no complaining, no power pushing. She wasn't used to it. At the hospital she had interned at in Houston, she'd been laughed at when she'd made a small suggestion and had been told to just follow the rules that someone much smarter than her had come up with years and years ago.

"I can come in early tomorrow and start on the organizational parts. I can write up the changes to help the other employees."

"Wonderful." He stood and handed the paper back to her. "I knew you were going to be good for us."

She smiled and took the paper from him. For the first time since entering the medical field, she felt like someone had listened to her opinions.

When she left the clinic, Alex was sitting in her truck waiting for her. She honked the horn and waved her over.

"So, how was your first day?" she asked.

"Crazy." Melissa smiled as she got into the truck.

"Busy. And the most wonderful day I've had in years." She smiled.

Alex laughed. "You belong here, sister," she said as she pulled out onto Main Street.

They chatted as Alex drove slowly through the small town. Much had changed since Melissa had left almost six years ago. The tornado that had ripped through town a little over a year ago had damaged most of the buildings in the older part of town. Now most of them had new storefronts and a fresh coat of paint. New streetlights and park benches lined the newly paved roads. The playground at the city park was bigger than ever.

The mayor, William Davis, a longtime Fairplay resident, had used the FEMA money well. Even the old movie theater was up and running now.

"I can't believe how much the town has grown."

Alex laughed. "Really?" She shrugged her shoulders. "I guess since I have never left, I can't see it, other than all the fixes after the tornado."

"It must have been hard when it hit."

Alex nodded. "We had some scary times, but everything turned out alright."

"Haley was hurt, wasn't she?" Haley and Melissa had been friends as kids and had spent the night at one another's houses at least once a month.

"Yeah, she broke her leg. She was banged up pretty good."

"I haven't gone out to see their new place yet." Melissa frowned and looked at her hands. "I guess I've been focusing on myself since getting into town."

"Don't worry about it. She has her hands full with those twins of theirs."

Melissa smiled, thinking of Haley and Wes's two boys. She'd bumped into Haley at the Grocery Stop and had cooed over the chubby boys. "They are so cute. I'll have to swing by their place and smother them with kisses again."

Alex laughed. "I can't believe she's the one that had twins. They run in the family, you know."

"Really?"

"Yeah, our grandfather was a twin, and we have twin cousins." She glanced over at her. "I think you met one of them at our wedding. Reece?"

"Hmm, I don't remember."

"He's tall, dark hair, green eyes, and had a sour look on his face the entire time." Alex smiled. "He's the younger one. Both boys had it hard growing up." She shook her head. "My aunt died young and their father was an ass. No one has heard from his brother, Ryan, in years." She shook her head and frowned.

"It must have been hard on them, losing their mother so young. I know Haley always talked about losing your mother. Then your dad died when we were fourteen and her grief started all over." She remembered that day. Haley had stopped spending the night at her house after that, and she had pulled away from their friendship. She'd always thought it was something she'd done or said to ruin the friendship. In the end, she'd become closer to her friend Holly, who now owned the local bookstore.

"Yeah, it hit her the hardest." Alex shook her head. "She was a daddy's girl. She was the only one of us that couldn't really remember our mother."

They drove through the gates of Grant and Alex's place, and Melissa looked at their lovely home. It sat down in a little valley. The large stone house sat off to the left and there was a big gray barn to the right. Her brother had so many animals, she had a hard time keeping up.

"What?" Alex asked when Melissa laughed.

"It's just that my brother has so many animals." She giggled again.

"What's so funny about that?"

"We never had any growing up. He knew how to ride, we both did, but now he owns horses, cows, chickens, and…" She giggled again. "Goats. I mean, he spoils those goats more than he does anything else."

"Tell me about it." Alex rolled her eyes and smiled. "They can do no wrong. Do you know that he's thinking of building a new barn, just for the goats?"

She nodded. "He told me over breakfast."

Alex grunted. "That man has a soft spot for those damn goats." She stopped the truck and turned to her with a smile on her face. "But, then again, so do I. Buttercup saved my life once, you know."

Melissa laughed. She'd heard the story of how the little goat had helped when Alex had been knocked out by Mrs. Nolan, the ex-mayor's wife.

"And Junior saved your brother." She nodded towards the large dog that hobbled across the yard to greet them.

The dog's thick dark fur hid the scars that everyone knew were there. Most of his left hind leg was so badly damaged, he spent most of his time lying down. Alex and Grant doted on the dog more than any other animal on their small farm.

"For that, we all owe him everything." Melissa knelt and rubbed the dog's thick fur as his tail thumped in the dirt. She got teary every time she thought about the scare they'd had after Mrs. Nolan had shot her brother point-blank. She'd spent almost a month at her parents' place until her brother had gotten back on his feet. The little dog had gotten the worst of it, though. And Mrs. Nolan was rotting away at some state-run loony bin in Rusk, Texas.

When she looked up, she saw her brother standing on the porch holding little Laura, as she liked to call her. They had named their daughter after Alex's mother, who had died in a tornado that hit Fairplay when the girls were very young.

She watched as Alex walked up and hugged and kissed her family. Something inside Melissa shifted and for the first time in her adult life, she wished for a moment just like that.

Lauren had given Reece the largest ranch house on the property. It had been sitting empty since they'd put in a few trailers closer to the barns. They had over a dozen men working for them now and, by the looks of it, they needed another dozen.

He'd spent the first day there helping with the cattle and had noticed a beautiful palomino running wild in one of the corrals. When he'd approached it, the beast's ears had perked up. Chase told him that the horse was still untrained and in dire need of breaking.

Chase hadn't had enough time to start working on the horse, and Reece had quickly requested the job.

"You can start on him first thing in the morning," Chase said, patting his back. "Just don't come running to me when the beast kills you. He's an ornery son of a gun."

He'd spent the rest of the day helping the hands brand

the cattle and getting the little ones up to date on shots. It had been a sweaty job, but he'd loved every minute.

When he got back to his place, he realized that the kitchen cupboards were completely empty, and he grabbed his truck keys to head down to the grocery store.

As he drove through the small town, he realized how much he felt at home here. They had visited often when they were kids. Up until their early teens, they had spent a few weeks here every summer to help out. He and his brother had made their best childhood memories here.

Pulling in front of the Grocery Stop, the only grocery store in town, he wondered how long he would stick around. He walked through the aisles, tossing items into his cart and thinking about breaking horses for a living. He'd always dreamed of being able to do that.

Maybe Fairplay was the place to do it. Why not? He knew a lot of people in town and, more important, they knew him. That was key for running a business like this. If they trusted him to do the job, he'd get more work. And there was bound to be a lot of work in these parts. They were less than an hour from Tyler, and there were plenty of smaller towns around that he could drum up business in.

"Well, well," he heard someone purr from behind him. "If it isn't one of the West boys."

He turned to see a busty blonde swaying down the aisle towards him. The tight shorts she wore barely covered her curves, and she was almost busting out of the shirt buttons. It took a few moments for his eyes to wander higher to see the well-groomed face that matched the perfect body.

He'd known Savannah Douglas most of her life. She'd been one of Lauren's best friends when they were younger, but after middle school, he'd seen less and less of her around the farm. She'd grown up in the lap of luxury ever since her folks had hit it big with oil money.

Now she wore the best clothes, drove the most expensive car in town, and was always after something she couldn't get.

He knew that Savannah was the cause of a lot of problems with his cousins over the last few years, but as she walked towards him, everything but the throbbing in his pants left his mind.

"Well, hello. This can't be little Savannah?" he said as she stopped right next to him.

"Which one are you?" She ran a manicured finger up his arm playfully.

"Reece." He smiled down at her.

"Oh, I could never tell you and your brother apart." She leaned closer to him. "I didn't know you were in town. How long are you here for?"

He could smell her perfume and the feel of her breasts pushed up against his chest was sending all his blood away from his head.

"Not sure. I'm thinking of staying on."

"For good?" She gasped a little. He could tell it was all an act, and if his mind had been working, he would have realized he shouldn't be leading her on. But it had been a while since he'd gotten any attention from someone so attractive.

"Maybe."

"Well, I'll simply have to bake you one of my famous pies and bring it over to you. Where are you staying?"

"At the ranch house at the end of the road at Lauren's place."

"Oh." She frowned a little.

"Problem?"

"No." Her smile came back. "Well, I'm sure we'll bump into each other again," she said, taking a step back when a young mother and her kids tried to get by them in the aisle. Savannah stared after the woman and kids. "I simply must be going." She leaned closer and whispered, "I'm looking forward to seeing you." Her eyes traveled up and down him and then rested on his crotch. If he were a teenager, he would have blushed bright red.

He watched her hips as she swayed back down the aisle and out the front door without buying anything.

"That girl is trouble," someone said from behind him.

When he turned around, he saw a very petite redheaded woman standing next to his cart, a full basket of groceries in her hands.

"Holly Bridles. We met at Alex and Grant's wedding and again at Haley and Wes'." She shifted her basket and held out a hand.

He smiled and took it. "I remember. You own a shop…" He tried to remember.

"Bookstore. It's just across the street."

"Right," he nodded, remembering.

"Savannah will toy with you. Besides, she's not allowed on Saddleback Ranch property anymore."

"Oh?" He must have looked surprised because Holly laughed.

"Long story. Ask your cousin one day if you have a few hours to listen to it. So did I hear you right? You're back to stay?"

"Maybe." He took her basket and set it inside his cart. The thing looked heavier than she did, and he could see she was struggling with it. "Why didn't you get a cart?"

"Oh, well, you know how it is. You run inside for one thing and…" She shrugged her shoulders. "You walk out with a cart full." She smiled.

They walked up to the checkout, and he put her basket up for her. They chatted for a while with the checker and when she had her two full bags in her arms, she turned back around to him. "Remember what I said about staying away from Savannah."

He nodded. "Thanks. I'll see you around."

She nodded and then turned and walked out.

"She's right, you know," the woman behind the counter said as she began scanning his items. "Everyone in town knows to steer clear of that girl."

He chuckled. "I think I'm getting the hint," he said, handing over his credit card. Until he could get the full story, Savannah Douglas was on his do-not-touch list.

CHAPTER 2

Reece flew through the air. Most people would be thinking about the pain they were about to feel when they hit the ground, but not him. His mind was completely and wonderfully blank. Of course, when he hit the ground hard, his mind started working again. What could he have done differently? Should he have nudged instead of poked? Should he have waited a few more days to try to mount the horse? So many questions popped into his head after he landed.

He hated it when he questioned himself. He was damn good at what he did, and he had the medals to prove it.

In the last five years, since he'd finally gotten free of his old man, he'd traveled the world and had collected as many medals as he could. Bronc busting had been his dream for as long as he could remember. But shortly after Reece had graduated, his old man had gotten sick. His no-good twin had gone and left him alone. They had always planned to leave together; at least that's what Reece had always thought.

Ryan had taken off, and Reece had made his own plans to leave. But then his dad had the stroke, and he'd been left caring for the old man until he finally passed away two years later. He'd also been left paying off all the old man's debts. He'd done everything he could to pay them off. He sold the cattle, the horses, then the land, and the house. Until he'd been left with only an old truck and a bag full of memories.

Then he'd given up his last hundred dollars to enter in the bronc busting competition at the rodeo, which, luckily, he'd won. He'd headed out to the next rodeo and won that one as well. He kept winning and eventually he was approached by a company just outside of New Orleans who wanted to sponsor him.

It had taken him almost a year to pay off his father's final debts, but by then he was so engrossed in bronc busting, he hadn't stopped.

It took the nasty fall in Montana to finally slow him down. Laid up in the hospital bed with a broken leg, three busted ribs, and a headache to rival all others, he'd finally thought about what he wanted to do with himself. He'd been injured before—he had pins in his right wrist, his left ankle, and had more stitches than he could count—but no other injury had affected him like this one had.

It took almost two months for him to finally make his way back to Texas. It hadn't been easy for him to drive up to Saddleback and ask his cousin for help.

Lauren had always been his favorite. She'd been more like a mother to Ryan and him than a cousin. She was only five years older than him but in so many ways, she was more mature. She'd been running Saddleback, the family ranch since she was eighteen.

When he'd driven up a few days ago, she'd rushed from the large front porch and hugged him so tight, he'd thought she'd cracked a few more of his ribs.

"What the hell have you done to yourself?" she'd asked as she pulled him into the house.

He'd laughed. "Fell off a damned horse."

She'd glared at him. "This is more than just falling off; this is getting stepped on a dozen times.

He'd smiled and nodded. "I guess that's about right."

"Reece Loyal West, what in the world am I going to do with you?"

"You could give me a place to stay until I'm back on my feet." She'd smiled and nodded.

"As long as you promise to stick around longer."

"I guess I can do that."

The next day, he'd moved into a large ranch-hand house they had along the back of their property.

He'd been at Alex's and Haley's weddings a few years back and had gotten to meet all of their husbands, but there were a few new editions that he'd yet to see.

He'd met Lauren and Chase's son, Rickie, but now they had an almost-one-year-old daughter, Emma, who was the spitting image of her mama.

That first night at dinner, Alex and Haley had brought their families over, and he'd met Alex's daughter, Laura, and Haley's twin boys, Conner and Cooper. He couldn't help but stare down at the matching boys' faces and think about his own twin. Where was Ryan? There was still a large hole in his life that his brother used to fill.

He'd gotten along great with Grant and Wes. He'd met all of them, including Lauren's husband, Chase, before.

Now here he was a few days later, working in the

corral and helping to break one of Chase's horses. Chase had warned him about jumping on the mare, but he hadn't listened. He'd wanted the feeling of excitement he got from riding hard and fast.

When he landed, though, he heard something snap and cussed himself for the fool he was.

"What on earth!" someone shouted. "Johnathan Chase Graham! Why would you let him get on Ralph?"

Ralph? Reece thought. Who the hell was Ralph?

"Now listen, Lauren, I tried my best to talk him out of it," Chase said, rushing over to him just as Lauren got there and gasped.

"He's bleeding."

He looked down at his leg and cussed. Sure enough, he'd busted the skin wide open just above his knee.

"It's nothing," he said, but he was quickly hushed by Lauren.

"Go pull the truck around. We'll have to drive him into the clinic." She helped him stand up as her husband rushed over to pull the truck closer to the corral.

"Why on heaven and earth would you get on a horse this soon?"

"I thought it was the right thing to do." He smiled down at her and winced with pain as he tried to use his recently healed leg.

"Did you break it again?" she asked, looking down at his torn jeans.

He tested it out and shook his head. "I don't think so."

"It would serve you right if you had." She helped him into the truck. "I'll drive him in; you can stay with the kids."

"No, I'll do it. It might take a while."

"Fine, but call me the second you hear anything," Lauren said, reaching over and snapping Reece's seat belt into place. She leaned up and placed a kiss on his cheek. "Dummy," she whispered before shutting the door. It was a nickname she'd always had for him. Ryan's nickname had been Dumber. He supposed he was lucky that she thought of his brother as dumber than he was.

Chase pulled out for the short ride into town.

"I'd like to start breaking horses. You know…as a business," Reese told him.

Chase laughed. "In your condition?"

"Well, maybe in a while. It's something I was always good at."

"Yeah, you looked really good flying through the air and landing on your face." Chase laughed.

"I'm just a little distracted, that's all."

"Well, when you get all healed, you're welcome to use the corral out in the east field. I don't think it's wise to keep too many new horses near the house."

He nodded. "Maybe I'll find a place of my own. I have some money saved up." He thought about all of his winnings, which he hadn't touched in three years. He didn't even know how much he had in the bank. After dealing with his father's debt, all that mattered to him was that there was a positive in front of the numbers instead of a negative.

"Grant could help you out there. He has some connections in town due to his business."

"Isn't he a lawyer?"

Chase laughed. "Yeah, but we don't hold it against him. He's the closest thing we have to a closing company in town. He knows all the listings and which people are looking to list their places."

"Maybe I'll check with him." He looked down at his leg and cussed as he watched blood squirting from his knee. "But I think it will have to wait a while." He could feel his head spinning and tried like crazy to hold onto consciousness.

"Damn it, don't you go passing out on me like a little girl." Chase shook his shoulder, but it was too late; everything had gone white.

When he opened his eyes again, he was looking into the biggest bluest eyes he'd ever seen. The woman's sandy blonde hair had fallen around her face, and she was looking down at him with concern. Without thinking, he reached up and brushed the strand of hair away from her face. He recognized the face instantly and smiled when she frowned down at him.

"Missy," he whispered.

"What have you done to yourself?" she asked, she looked away as someone else spoke to her, and he instantly wanted her blue eyes back on him.

His mind drifted until he heard the word, "shots." Then he sat up.

"I don't need any shots." When he tried to get off the table, she pushed down on his shoulders until he lay back down.

"You will stay put until I tell you to move. Is that clear?" Her blue eyes turned fierce.

"Yes, ma'am." He lay back down and closed his eyes. He heard her ask Chase a few questions, and then she asked him to wait outside in the waiting room while she examined Reece, which got his mind thinking in all different kinds of directions.

It had been a while, almost five months, since he'd been with a woman. Who could blame him for the thoughts he was having now?

"Can you remove your pants, or do I need to cut them off of you?"

He looked up at those blue eyes and just smiled until he saw her cheeks flush. "I think I can manage."

"Good." She handed him a standard hospital robe. He hated these damn things.

"Can't you just patch me up while I keep my pants on?"

"No," she said as she put things onto the silver tray in front of him.

He stood up to yank his pants down, and the room began to spin again. Cussing under his breath, he closed his eyes and tried to steady himself. When he felt her cool hands on his hips, his eyes flew open. She tugged his torn jeans down his legs until they got hung up on his boots, and then she pushed him lightly until he sat back down on the table.

"How'd I get in here? Please don't tell me Chase carried me like a baby?"

He enjoyed the rich giggle that escaped her lips. "No, we moved you to a gurney." She nodded to the rolling bed that was sitting against the wall.

She pulled one of his boots off and reached for the other one.

"I'd better do that one. I have a few pins in that ankle that hurt when it's pulled too much." She nodded and stood back, watching him.

He bent down and, using his other foot, managed to pry the boot loose.

She set the boots on a chair by the door. When she turned back around, her eyes roamed over his now bare legs. When he handed her his jeans, she hesitated.

"Get injured often?" she asked, looking at the many scars he had on his legs.

He shrugged his shoulders. "Comes with busting."

She shook her head. "Sounds like you need a new job," she said as she started working on his knee.

He tried not to look at the nasty gash and focused on her instead. Her hair was darker than he remembered. He'd met her a few times, most recently at Alex's wedding where he'd quickly developed a huge crush on her. He had seen her from across the room and had wanted to rush over and ask her out. But she'd had a date, a skinny black-haired guy with glasses, which had reminded him that he had a date as well. His date was blonde and busty, and their relationship lasted only three weeks, one of his longest relationships to date.

"When did you move back?" he asked, wishing he could reach out and touch her silky hair again. When he'd seen her last, she was living in the city attending college.

"Two months ago," she said as she cleaned his knee. She looked up from his knee for a moment. "When did you get into town?"

"A few days ago. I'm staying with Lauren and Chase until I can find a place of my own."

He watched her eyebrows go up in a sexy arch.

"I'm over at Alex and Grant's. You're here to stay then?"

He shrugged his shoulders. "Until I can think of someplace else to be. How about you? Are you here to stay?"

She nodded and got back to work cleaning the dirt from his wound. "Until I can think of someplace else to be."

He winced when she pulled a large pebble from under his skin.

"Sorry," she said.

"It's okay."

"Do you pass out every time you see blood?" she asked, casually.

He looked up at her and winced. He hated the weakness. "So far."

"Chase told me that you'd been injured recently."

"Yeah, a couple of broken ribs, broken leg." He shrugged. "For the most part, I'm healed."

"Most part?" Her eyebrows did the sexy arch again.

"I'm walking around just fine. Still breathing."

"Mr. West," she began.

"Reece," he corrected.

She shook her head and continued. "If you continue to treat your body like it's a plaything instead of a well-oiled machine, you won't be using it much longer." She tossed the tweezers on the tray, picked up a threaded needle, and began to place tiny stitches into his skin.

"Are you a doctor?" He frowned, causing her to pause.

"No." She frowned back at him. "The doctor is away at lunch. Would you like to wait an hour and have Dr. Conner put these in instead?"

"No, it's just that…" He trailed off. "No, ma'am."

She nodded and got back to work. She was fast and very efficient, and her stitches looked better than those he'd received from some of the best doctors around. She placed a white bandage over the wound.

She examined his leg, moving her hands gently over his hairy muscles. It was pure torture to sit still. She finally nodded and said, "You'll need to stay off your leg for a few hours. No horseback riding for at least a week. You can come back then and we'll remove the stitches. Take a few aspirins when you get home."

"Yes, ma'am." He was already thinking about riding again when she tugged on his sleeve.

"I mean it, Reece. No riding until I say so." She frowned at him.

"Go out with me this weekend," he blurted out. Normally he didn't just bark out a date request. Maybe it was the pain blocking his normally smooth personality.

She looked at him and a small smile formed on her lips.

"I don't date patients, Mr. West." She turned around and tossed him his pants. "You're free to go." She looked at him one last time and then walked out of the room, leaving him wishing he hadn't fallen off the damn horse.

Melissa walked into her small office and leaned against the closed door. Her fingers were still shaking and when she tried to calm her heart down, she felt it jump in her chest.

What had she done? Why had she turned him down? Reece West was the sexiest man she'd met in a long time. Why, oh why, hadn't she noticed how sexy he was at her brother's wedding? Shaking her head clear, she remembered she'd been in a relationship at the time and frowned.

Now it was best for her to focus on her work. In the last few months, she'd turned the little clinic around. They were saving money and getting patients through faster and more efficiently.

Dr. Conner—Chris, as he wanted her to call him—had asked her out on several occasions. Each time she'd politely informed him that she didn't date coworkers. She was beginning to wonder why she was making so many excuses to get out of going on a date. After all, it was just a date.

Just as she picked up a folder to glance at the next patient information, her office door opened. She looked up through her reading glasses as Reece walked into her office with a smile on his face.

"I like the specs," he said as he walked over and sat in the chair opposite her.

"Mr. West, maybe I didn't make myself clear. You are free to go."

"Oh, you were very clear about that. Just not the other issue." He leaned back and crossed his arms over his chest.

"Other issue?" She removed her glasses and was surprised when he frowned a little as she placed them on the desk beside her.

"Why you wouldn't go out on a date with me. After all, when you live in a town of three thousand people, everyone's bound to be a patient of yours at one point or another."

She frowned. He was right, and she hated to admit it.

"Have you ever thought that maybe I just don't want to go out with you?"

He shook his head. "Not with the way you were looking at me back there with my pants off." He nodded towards the door and smiled. "What harm would it do? It's just a date."

She'd just told herself the same thing less than a minute ago, and she couldn't lie to herself—she was very attracted to him. So much so, that her hands started to shake again, and she pushed them under the desk and nodded.

"Fine, one date." She watched his lips turn up into a sexy grin.

"Great." He got up, and she noticed that he winced a little.

"Do you need help?" She was beside him in an instant. Her arms wrapped around his narrow waist, and she held him steady so he wouldn't fall.

When he held still, she looked up into his face and realized she'd walked right into his trap. She was exactly where he wanted her to be—in his arms. When she tried to pull away, he shook his head and frowned.

"No, hang on a sec." He dipped his head and when his lips met hers, she felt her toes curl and the wind was knocked from her lungs.

He took his time exploring her lips, softly running his over hers until she sighed and opened her mouth to his exploration.

She didn't know how long they stood there like that, but when he finally released her, they were both breathless.

"Friday, six o'clock," he said softly.

She couldn't speak, so instead, she nodded and watched him slowly walk out. She noticed the slight limp as he made his way down the hallway towards the waiting area.

Closing the door, she rested her forehead against the cool wood and sighed. She was in trouble.

Then she realized she really *was* in trouble. It had been almost a year since she'd been on a date with anyone. She had absolutely nothing to wear.

Rushing over to her desk, she picked up her office phone and dialed the bookstore. Holly had taken over the small store when her mother had retired to Florida. Books were Holly's life. That and fashion.

Her friend not only knew all the latest trends, she wore them. You wouldn't know it to look at the slight, red-haired bookseller, but the girl was a whirlwind at putting outfits together. Not only clothes but hair and make-up as well.

"Holly, it's Melissa. I need your help. I've got a date this Friday and I need your fashion help."

"Who with?" Holly broke in.

"Reece West."

"Ohhhhh."

"I know. Oh my God! Why didn't anyone tell me how sexy the man was?" She leaned back in her chair and remembered how he had looked in his boxer shorts and shirt.

"You've met the West twins before. At least I think you have. Well, anyway, I'm sure I've mentioned them tons of times."

Melissa shook her head. "I don't remember."

"Oh, well…" Holly sighed. "I ran into Reece yesterday at the Grocery Stop. My, oh, my. Anyway, swing by the bookstore after closing and you can tell me all. We'll come up with something for Friday."

"Sounds great. I'll see you then." She had a hard time

concentrating the rest of the day. Her lips still vibrated from the kiss. Every time she had a moment to herself, she found herself daydreaming about Reece.

Finally, at a quarter after six, she walked out the front door of the clinic and waved bye to the night shift nurse, Kimberly.

She walked the four blocks to the bookstore instead of driving. The weather was finally getting warm enough that she didn't have to put on her light jacket.

When she walked into the bookstore, the bell chimed above the door. Holly served cappuccinos and baked goods as well as selling books and small novelty items. There was a line of regulars that had stopped by the place to get their latte fix and some of the best banana walnut bread anywhere. Holly had received the recipe from her mother along with the business.

The place was large. The building owner had rebuilt the front of the store after the tornado had wiped it out, but much of the place was still out of date. Holly had mentioned that she was working out a plan with the current owner about doing some more updates, but Melissa thought she should just find another building.

"Hi," Holly said from behind the counter.

"Hi. Busy day?" She looked around the store and saw several people browsing the aisles.

"It was great for a Wednesday. You?"

She shrugged her shoulders. "The usual. Bumps, cuts, and bruises. Mr. MacKalaster came in with a broken finger. Apparently, his cat slammed the piano top on it when he was playing."

Holly giggled. "Do you remember how many hours we spent pounding away at those keys during practice?"

"I know. How many times did we wish we could break his fingers because he would tap our knuckles with a ruler when we hit the wrong key?"

They giggled, then sobered. "Well, that's too bad. I hope he will make a speedy recovery," Holly said, looking around the store.

"Yes." Melissa cleared her throat, knowing it wouldn't do to have the head nurse at the local clinic laughing about someone's injuries. "Well, it was just his middle finger." She giggled again and tried to cover it up with a cough.

Holly smiled. "It's almost closing time. Why don't I grab you a latte and you can look through some of these magazines to help you get an idea of what you want to wear?"

She nodded. "I'll have a piece of banana bread too if you have any left."

Holly smiled. "I saved you a piece."

CHAPTER 3

By the time Reece walked into his place later that night, he felt like he'd been kicked in the chest instead of knocked off a horse. His leg hurt like a hell, and he was covered in sweat and dust.

He'd been told to stay off a horse, but not to steer clear of the creatures. Breaking horses was much more than just plopping down on their backs and holding on. It took weeks, sometimes months, of getting an animal to trust you. You had to teach them how to be on a lead, how to take a bit in their mouths and not bite your fingers while they were at it. He looked down at his bruised thumb and frowned.

Then you had to get them used to the weight of the blanket and saddle. He sat down on the sofa and sighed, wishing too late that he'd thought of grabbing a cold beer from his fridge. Pulling himself off the sofa, he walked into the kitchen and popped the top off a Corona Light.

Everyone gave him shit about drinking light beer and

stopping after one, but he didn't mind. He actually enjoyed the taste a lot better.

Opening up the back sliding door, he stepped out onto the back deck and leaned against the railing. The sun was just setting over the hills and the fields had turned a dark shade of amber. The night sky had yet to turn dark, reminding him of the sexy blue eyes which had looked at him with such concern earlier that day.

He looked down at his torn jeans and noticed that the white bandage was now covered in dirt and sweat. He knew he would have to replace it after he showered and wished that Melissa was here to do the job for him. He didn't know why he turned into a baby when he saw blood, but he'd done everything he could over the last few years to avoid looking at it, including having someone else dress his wounds.

When the sun finally dipped below the hills, he went inside, peeled off his clothes, and threw them in the hamper. He walked to the bathroom, turned on the shower, and stepped in.

He had hoped that the hot water would remove the bandage for him, but when he stepped out half an hour later, the tape was still stuck to his thigh.

"Damn." He sat on the edge of the tub and started to peel the tape aside. When it was finally removed, along with half of the hair on his leg, he looked at the small stitches. Nine of them. Since she'd cleaned most of the blood, he didn't feel the weakness come over him like he normally did.

He pulled open the shopping bag full of bandages he and Chase had purchased earlier. Ripping a box open, he grabbed the biggest bandage and put it over the cut and smiled at the job well done.

The next morning, he found it very hard to get out of bed. Every muscle in his body ached. It had been a while since he'd spent a full day working like he'd done yesterday. And then he'd been thrown from a horse on top of it all.

Three months. Three long months now since he'd been tossed around like a rag doll and stepped on repeatedly by that horse in Montana. Five years ago, it would have taken him half this time to be back on his feet, but now…He stood and looked at himself in the mirror and frowned. He was getting old. Why was twenty-five feeling like thirty-five? He looked down at the row of scars that ran over his chest and legs. Battle scars. Some were so small; he'd forgotten he had them. Others, like the one over his outer thigh, which he now ran his fingertips over, were a lot bigger and meaner and he remembered every pain-filled moment.

Tossing on some clean jeans and a shirt, he pulled his boot on over the compression sock he wore on his left ankle. When he rode, he wore one on his wrist, elbow, and knees. They seemed to help his achy joints.

When he walked up to the big barn, Chase was out front working with the horse from yesterday.

"Did I hear your wife call this beauty Ralph yesterday?"

Chase chuckled. "Yeah. Your cousins have a way with naming animals."

"Tell me about it." He shook his head and started to climb into the corral.

"Oh, no, you don't." Alex walked down from the front

porch. "I heard about your spill yesterday." She stopped right in front of him. "Don't think for a moment that I'm going to let you mess around with my horse for a while." She pointed at his chest.

"Your horse?" He looked at Chase and laughed. "Ralph here is yours?"

"Yes. Why?" She frowned.

"It's just..." He broke off and sobered when Chase shook his head quickly. "Nothing."

"What?" she asked, crossing her arms over her chest.

"He's a beast. How do you expect that you'll ever ride him? I mean, he's over four years old and hasn't been broken."

"I know." She walked over to the fence and smiled at the animal, who Chase was running on a lead. "He's beautiful, isn't he?" She glanced at Reece.

"Well, yes. Tell me he's a gift for Grant."

She shook her head no. "He's all mine."

"Alex..." He walked over and took her shoulders. "That horse has too much spunk for you. He'll end up killing you. You have a baby now. Why don't you pick a nice quiet older horse?" He nodded to one that was standing along the fence with its eyes closed. "Like that one."

Alex looked and then laughed. "I'm a mother, not dead. Besides, that's Dash, Haley's horse. Laura can crawl faster than he can run."

He looked at the old beast. "That's Dash? I thought he died years ago."

"Nope, still kicking around." She smiled. "He's going to live to be a zillion years old. Haley told me." She smiled and sighed, looking back at the beautiful palomino running in circles. "I've wanted Ralph here for years. Mr. Hobby had him up on the dairy farm, and I would drive by every week and watch him run." She rested her foot up on the bottom rung next to his.

"I still don't think it's a great idea. I mean, this horse is better suited for busting."

She glared at him. "I thought you were done with busting?"

He shook his head. "I'll never be done with it."

"We had hoped that you would be." She nodded towards the horse. "I've seen you at your best and I can't deny that you have a way with horses. But I've also seen you at your worst. You've some recovering to do yet." She closed her eyes and then turned to him. "You've broken a lot of horses in your day. What do you honestly think?" She nodded to the horse that was bucking around the small corral.

He'd seen the fire in its eyes and felt it quiver under him and knew what the horse wanted. It had too much spirit to become someone's ride. "He's meant for busting. We could break him. It would take some doing"—he looked at Alex again— "but he was meant to be wild."

She sighed, and he saw her shoulders hunch a little. "I had hoped…" She shook her head and he watched a tear escape her eyes. "You'll be the first to ride him?" She rested her hand on his, her brown eyes pleading.

He smiled and nodded. "When we're both ready."

She was a wreck. She'd gone into Tyler and gotten her hair colored and had a manicure and pedicure to boot. It had been almost a full year since she'd splurged on herself. It would have been better had Holly or Haley been able to go with her, but Holly was busy with her bookstore and Haley with the twins. But both of her friends had promised to have a girls' night soon.

She'd even stopped off at the mall and gotten some new clothes. Thanks to the pictures Holly had shown her, it was easy to pick out the colors and styles that looked great on her.

She stood looking at herself in the mirror, and while she thought she looked absolutely gorgeous, she felt like a wreck on the inside. She was so nervous; she didn't think she could go through with the evening.

Someone knocked on her door and she turned to see Alex walk in with the baby on her hip.

"Don't you look perfect." She smiled and walked over to her. "That color blue goes perfectly with your eyes. Oh!" she exclaimed making the sleepy baby in her arms squirm, "look at those shoes." She tilted her head and smiled. "I miss wearing shoes like that." Her smile turned into a slight frown.

"Sounds like someone needs some mommy and daddy time. Maybe Aunt Melissa can babysit one night?" she said brushing a strand of blonde hair away from her niece's eyes.

"I'd love some mommy and daddy time." Alex smiled at her.

"Who gets mommy and daddy time?" Grant asked from the doorway as he walked over and took the baby from his wife and then planted a kiss on her chubby cheek.

"We do. Your sister is going to babysit sometime so we

can hit the town." Alex did a little dance. "I'll get to wear sexy shoes again."

He smiled. "I like your boots, but a date night would be great." Then he turned to Melissa. "Wow, sis. Lookin' good."

She smiled. "Thanks." Just then the doorbell rang and the butterflies jumped in her stomach. "Why am I so nervous?" she groaned.

Alex chuckled. "Because you're going out with a West. We've been known to make a few hearts flutter." She smiled and rushed to answer the door.

"Should I be worried?" Grant asked, shifting Laura. The baby was now completely asleep in her daddy's arms.

"No. Of course not. It's just a date." She brushed her brother off, but she was worried about herself.

It wasn't as if she hadn't dated before. She'd been in a long-term relationship during her first year at college. But compared to Reece, Bret had been a boy.

When she'd seen Reece standing across from her in nothing but his boxers, her mouth had watered. She'd never seen a man look so good in boxer briefs before. His thighs were thick, and his dark skin was covered in a light dusting of dark hair. The scars that marred his skin weren't bad, but noticeable. His green eyes had been something to see, and she'd been drawn in the second he'd opened them. She couldn't explain it, but somehow, they were familiar to her. Like a memory pushed to the back of her mind.

When she walked down the stairs with Grant behind her, she was shocked to see how handsome Reece looked in dress pants and a button-up shirt. His hair was darker than she'd first thought, possibly because last time she'd seen him he'd had a layer of dust covering him. It was brushed back away from his face, setting off the West green eyes. The fact that he looked just as good wearing torn jeans and a mangled shirt with a layer of dirt covering him as he did in dress pants and a starched shirt didn't go unnoticed.

"Evening." She watched his eyes heat when he noticed her on the stairs.

"Hi." She smiled and felt like a teenager going on her first date.

"You look lovely." He walked over to her and placed a soft kiss on her cheek. That's when Grant cleared his throat.

"Evening, Grant." He walked over and shook her brother's hand. Grant shifted his daughter and easily took Reece's hand.

"Evening. I heard you had some excitement with my wife's horse the other day. I've been telling her since she got that horse that it wasn't meant for riding."

He smiled. "I think we got it all worked out." He winked at Alexis.

"Reece has purchased Ralph from me. He's going to ride him for busting."

"You're what?" Melissa said before she could stop herself. "Are you just plain stupid?"

Reece laughed. "Some days." He took her hand and started walking towards the door. "Evening." He dipped his head towards Grant and Alex and continued to walk with her out the front door.

"Well?" She pulled him to a stop just before his truck.

"Well, what?" he asked, taking a step closer to her.

"Are you really going to continue bronc busting?"

"Yes, ma'am, I am. I'll get back to it as soon as my

doctor and nurse clear me." He smiled and ran his finger down her cheek. She tried to hide the shiver of excitement that ran through her. "You must have a death wish." It came out as a whisper.

"Nope, just a powerful urge to be bucked off something." He smiled and stepped back to open her door for her.

She glared at him as he helped her up into his truck. While he walked around the front, she tried to mentally switch gears. It wouldn't do any good to be angry at him all the way through their first date.

"How's the leg?" she asked as he got behind the wheel.

"Pretty good. I changed the bandage the other day without passing out." He smiled over at her.

"That's always good. How long have you fought with vasovagal episodes?"

"Vaso…what?"

"Fainting at the sight of blood?" She smiled.

"Oh, since I was a kid, I guess. My brother got thrown off a buck once, skinned his back up pretty good. Since our pa wasn't too keen on fixing us up, I had to do it. I remember standing over him with a washcloth in one hand and medicine in the other. Next thing I knew, Ryan was kicking me in my ribs and yelling at me. I never lived it down." He shook his head and smiled as he drove out of town.

"You two must have been close."

"Yeah," he shrugged. "I guess."

"Alex told me that no one has heard from him in a few years. It must be hard being away from him for so long."

"I guess." He glanced over at her. "What was it like going to school in Houston?"

It was her turn to shrug her shoulders and glance out the window. "It had its ups and downs. I interned at Children's for a semester." She closed her eyes and remembered some of the better moments she'd had. She chose to think about those rather than the harder times, the times she had to say goodbye to children so small, so helpless.

"I don't know how you all do it." He shook his head. "Staying calm as someone's bleeding out."

"I guess it's the same way you can square off with a very angry thousand-pound beast."

He shrugged. "I guess so."

During their drive into Tyler, there was never a lull in the conversation, and Reece enjoyed every minute of their time together. She made him laugh and think, which no other women he'd dated had been able to do.

He'd dated a lot during his travels. Most of the women had been buckle bunnies, and he had always enjoyed the pick of the prettiest ones. But he hadn't wanted to spend time with any of them the way he did with Melissa.

He listened to her talk about her experiences at the hospitals in Houston and about things she'd done as a child. When she asked him questions, he tried to avoid giving up too much information, since there wasn't anything really exciting about his life. But when he started to talk about his time at the rodeo, she leaned forward, her plate of food completely forgotten as she listened to every word.

"That's how I ended up with the pins in my foot."

She shook her head at him. "What did you do with the horse?"

He laughed. "A year later I got right back on him and rode him across the field then sold him immediately to the man down the street."

She nodded her head. "Good move."

"What about you? Do you ride?"

She shrugged her shoulders then picked up her glass of wine and took a sip. "I've ridden, but I'm not very good at it."

He leaned back in his chair and looked at her. "I doubt that. You have grace about you. I'd bet you'd be good in the saddle." Her face turned a light shade of pink and she smiled.

"My brother is the one that likes all the animals."

"What do you say I take you riding next week? That is after I clear it with my nurse."

He was dying to see her in tight jeans and boots, bouncing up and down in a saddle.

"Well…"

"You're bound to have a day off from work."

She nodded. "Oh, yes, of course. Fridays, Saturdays, and Sundays are all mine. At least most of the time." She smiled.

"Good. Then it's settled. What do you say to a picnic next Friday?"

She thought about it for a moment and then nodded her head.

The drive back to Fairplay was a quiet one. Not the scary silent type where he felt like there should be something said, but instead a peaceful one where nothing needed to be said. He enjoyed the rolling hills as he took the curve towards town.

"I talked to a realtor the other day about finding a place," he said out of the blue after seeing a for-sale sign for some land.

"Oh?" She sighed and looked out the window. "I've been putting off moving out of my brother's place since I got here. What kind of place are you looking for?"

"Something with some land. I want to continue breaking horses. I've been doing it since I was twelve."

"Twelve?" She glanced over at him.

"Yeah. My father thought that we should start earning our keep early on." He wanted to change the subject quickly, so he asked, "What kind of place are you looking for?"

"Just an apartment. There are a few places in town, but so far I haven't found anything I like."

"I saw a sign at the big white house right inside of town."

"The Nolan place?" She squinted. "Yeah, I guess they have an apartment above their garage."

"That's the Nolan place?" He remembered how Mrs. Nolan had shot Melissa's brother and kidnapped his cousin Alex.

"Yeah, but Patty is still locked up. Roy used to be the mayor. Maybe I'll stop by and take a look at the place."

"Really?" He glanced over at her. "You'd rent a place from the man whose wife almost killed your brother?"

"Roy has nothing to do with the sickness his wife has," she said, glaring at him.

"No, of course not, but..." He shrugged his shoulders.

If she could get over something like that than she was a better person than he was.

"What?" she asked, crossing her arms over her chest and waiting for him to speak.

"Nothing." He smiled over at her.

"Besides, I know for a fact that it's a pretty good-sized apartment."

"How do you know that?"

She shrugged her shoulders and looked out the window. "I went out with their son once."

"You went out with Travis? Alex's ex-fiancé?"

"Sure, it was during one of their break-ups. Alex knows all about it." She looked out the window again.

The thought of Melissa and Travis together had his stomach turning for some reason.

When they finally pulled up in front of her brother's place, he desperately wished she had a place of her own so she could invite him in. The front porch light was on, but the rest of the house was dark.

"I had a really wonderful time," she said as she started to reach for the door handle. He stopped her by putting his hand on her arm and pulling her towards him. When he took her mouth, he thought he heard her moan. Maybe he had made the sound since her fingers were digging into his shoulders and holding him close.

When he finally pulled back, he smiled when he heard her breathing hitch a little. She reached for the door again.

He stopped her a second time. "My mother died when I was young, but she still taught me some of the more important values in life." When she tilted her head and looked at him questioningly, he laughed. "Missy, let me open the door for you." She smiled and nodded. He got out and walked around his truck and helped her down. He held her close until her feet hit the dirt driveway. Her body felt so good up against his, he didn't want to let her go.

"I'll see you next Friday," he whispered before giving her a light kiss.

She nodded and smiled back, and he watched her walk up the porch and into the house.

When he got back in his car, he couldn't have stopped the smile on his face if he'd wanted to. For the first time since his brother had left him, he was feeling like he had someone he could talk to, and it felt great.

CHAPTER 4

"Why do I have to have a new cast?" Libby Jackson, one of Melissa's favorite patients, was asking. The little girl was holding her right arm against her chest and frowning up at her through thick glasses.

"Because your arm isn't healed yet." She leaned down and looked at the little girl in the eyes. "But, this one you can pick the color of."

The girl's eyes got a little bigger. "You mean it won't be white?"

Melissa shook her head. "I have six colors you can choose from. Would you like to see them before the doctor comes in?"

Libby nodded her head.

Ten minutes later, as the doctor wrapped the little girl's arm in a bright green cast, Melissa stood by and talked to Libby's mother, Cara.

"Thank you. I didn't know how to tell her that she'd

have to have cast on for a few more weeks. She hated the last one so much."

Melissa smiled. "I remember having a cast on when I was about her age." She shook her head remembering the nuisance. "This one will be lighter and a lot smaller than the first one. Maybe it won't be so bad for her."

"I hope so. It's hard enough that she's hasn't gotten to play with her brothers in the last few weeks, but now that school has started, she's not allowed to play on the play-ground until the cast comes off."

"Oh, well, that doesn't seem fair."

Cara shrugged her shoulders. "School rules. Until she gets a clean bill of health, they don't want her re-injuring herself."

"I guess that makes sense," Melissa said, frowning down at the little girl. Still, part of her thought it was unfair to keep the little girl inside while all her friends got to play.

Then she remembered Reece. Hadn't she just told him the same thing a few days ago? No riding horses until his leg was healed. It was just a scratch. A scratch that had to have nine stitches. She shook her head clear and tried to concentrate for the rest of the day. She'd found herself thinking about Reece a lot in the three days since their date.

In those days, she'd finally settled on a place of her own and had signed the lease on a small greenhouse just a few blocks from the clinic. The place belonged to Sheriff Miller, but ever since he'd moved in with Jamella, the place had sat empty. He'd overheard her making a call from the diner about an apartment for rent and had told her right there that she was welcome to his place for whatever price she could afford. She'd been hesitant at first until he'd told her that the place was already furnished and that she could do whatever other decorating that she saw fit.

After getting a quick tour of the house, she'd given him a check and had settled on moving in the following day.

When she'd asked Dr. Conner for the day off, he had quickly replied yes and asked if she needed help moving in. She'd told him no since all she had were a few items that she'd put in storage in her brother's garage. What she really needed was someone to do some shopping with her at the secondhand store, since she needed a few other amenities.

Since Alex was busy that day, she'd called Haley and asked if she wanted to do some shopping.

The next morning when she walked downstairs, she was happy to see Haley and the twins in the kitchen eating breakfast already.

"Good morning." Her friend looked up at her with a smile. Haley hadn't changed in years. Her long dark hair still hung below her shoulders with a light wave, and her rich green eyes still sparkled with mischief. And even after giving birth to two very healthy boys, she still had a figure Melissa would have killed for.

"Morning. How are my two favorite boys this morning?" She walked over to the highchairs and kissed both of the chubby cheeks as the boys plowed Cheerios into their mouths.

"Well, Conner decided he was going to spill all his juice instead of drink it, and Cooper thought it was great fun and joined in." She stood up and Melissa saw the large stain on Haley's shirt. She tried not to laugh, but since Haley had a large smile on her face, she couldn't help it.

"I'm sure I have a shirt that would fit you upstairs."

"Don't worry." Haley bent down and pulled out a shirt from the enormous baby bag sitting next to her on the floor. "I come prepared. Would you mind watching them while I run up and change?" She looked down at the soaked shirt, sniffed, and frowned. "Maybe I'll shower while I'm at it."

Melissa laughed. "I'd love to. Take your time." She leaned over and picked up one of the boys. She thought it was Conner, but she had a hard time telling them apart.

Haley started to walk out of the room but looked back over her shoulder at her. "That's Cooper." She nodded to the boy in Melissa's arms and then smiled and left.

"Well, Cooper." She looked down at the boy who was trying to pull her earrings out of her ears. "What do you say we see about cleaning you two up?"

It took longer than she thought possible to get both the boys' hands and faces cleaned from the gummy Cheerios.

"How is it"—she blew a strand of her blonde hair out of her face— "that you two can make such a huge mess with just Cheerios?"

She was sitting on the kitchen floor. Cooper was cleaned up and playing with a stack of blocks while she tried to clean up Conner. But the second boy was having none of the warm washcloth. The chubby kid could fight like a pro. His little legs and arms flailed about, causing her to almost drop him several times. That's when she sat on the floor, just in case.

"Awww, is there a price of admission for the show?" someone said from behind her.

She gasped and looked quickly over her shoulder to see Reece standing in the back doorway, his arms crossed over his chest and his boots resting against the door frame.

"Don't just stand there." She turned back to the wiggly kid in her arms. "Come to give me a hand." She heard him laugh as he sat next to her on the kitchen rug.

Upon seeing Reece, Conner quickly threw his hands up towards him and started begging. Melissa let the kid crawl across her lap towards Reece, where he plopped down in his lap and leaned his messy face on Reece's clean shirt.

"There," Reece said, stroking the kid's dark hair. "The torture ends." He smiled up at her as Conner's big eyes looked at her with distaste.

"Well, really." She crossed her arms over her chest. "I'll have you know that Cooper cooperated just fine. Didn't you?" She leaned over and picked up the happy kid who was now chewing on a large block.

"Maybe all he needed was another man," Reece said, rocking the kid gently back and forth in his arms.

"You would think that he'd take a hint from his brother."

Reece shook his head. "Conner is his own man." He smiled down at the boy's face. "He's shy and doesn't like to be forced, whereas Cooper is more relaxed and just goes with whatever is going on." Reece looked over at the boy in her arms. "They're as different as Ryan and I were."

"How can you tell them apart?" she asked looking between the boys. "Other than the fact that Conner won't let me touch him."

"Cooper has a small freckle on his chin. Ryan had a

scar above his left eye that I was told I gave him when we were in diapers." He reached over and brushed the small spot on Cooper's chin, which Melissa wouldn't have noticed otherwise. "Conner here"—he rubbed the little boy's legs— "is a daddy's boy and is always wearing Cowboy socks."

Melissa looked down and noticed the Dallas Cowboy socks on the boy. When she looked down at Cooper, she noticed he was wearing red and blue Houston Texans socks.

"It's an ongoing fight between Haley and Wes." He chuckled.

"Really?" She smiled and when Haley walked in, she asked her about it.

Haley laughed. "Yes, it's also my way of telling the two apart." Her smile fell away. "But if you tell their father that, I'll deny it."

Melissa laughed. "Are you ready?"

"Yes, all cleaned. At least until they decide to throw more food at me." She reached over and took Cooper from her, giving him playful kisses on his chubby cheeks. The boy's laughter was contagious.

"Where are you two…four, off to today?"

"Shopping," Haley broke in. "Missy's rented Sheriff Miller's place. She moves in tomorrow."

"Sheriff Miller moved?" He frowned, trying to remember where the man lived.

"Now that he's living with Jamella, the old place downtown is empty. It'll be good to have someone in it again," Haley said, putting Cooper into his carrying seat. The kid played with the toys dangling down in front of his face.

"Is it the dark green place on the corner of Magnolia and Center Way?"

"Yes. I couldn't believe my luck when I bumped into the Sheriff," Melissa said.

He started to put Conner into his matching seat, but Conner was having none of it.

Haley took the wiggly boy from him. "You have to bribe him." She pulled out a cracker from her bag and handed it to him. "There, now we're all ready." She picked up one carrier then moved to grab the other one.

"Hold on there, Xena." Reece grabbed the carrier before she could break her back. "Sometimes you just need to ask for help."

He helped them out to Haley's SUV and Melissa was happily shocked when he leaned over and kissed her on the lips right in front of his cousin. She tried not to look out the side mirror at the image he made standing in front of the big barn, his worn jeans ripped at the knee and his Stetson low on his head. Damn, she was in trouble.

"Sooooo," Haley said as they pulled out of the driveway. "Are you going to tell me all the juicy details?"

Melissa laughed. "There aren't any…yet." She relaxed in her seat and prepared to enjoy a day shopping with a good friend.

Reece stood in the dirt and looked at the little patch of green land. He knew with some sweat; he could make it work for him. The house that sat in the middle of the twenty acres needed some TLC, but it would keep the rain off his head. The question was, could he afford it?

In the last few days, he'd checked and rechecked his bank account. At first, he thought there had been a mistake, but after the clerk told him his balance for the third time, he realized that years of being on the circuit had been kind to him.

He was sitting on enough money to buy a piece of land, maybe even one with a house on it, and he might still have enough left over to get a couple horses of his own. He turned to the realtor, Mike Coalfield, who had driven him out to the place a few miles outside of Fairplay.

"What're they asking?"

The man looked down at his nails and sighed. "Well, here's where we might hit a snag. The Joneses want one-eighty, but I've been telling them that the most they'll get is one-fifty.

He calculated in his head and nodded. "Make an offer for one-forty-five." He turned and looked out across the land again.

"Are you sure? You don't want to look at the house some more before you make up your mind?"

"The land is where I'll be most. Besides"—he turned and looked at the four-bedroom ranch home— "I can tell the place has good bones. Anything else can be fixed."

"It's your dime." He shook his head and started walking towards his car. "It'll take a few days. The Joneses are in Florida now. Went off and retired and are living the dream."

Reece shook his head. "The dream is right here." He nodded to the field and smiled when the sun chose that moment to peek out from behind a cloud, blanketing the grass in its bright light.

He drove back into town after signing a few papers at

the realtor's office and decided that a celebratory dinner was in order. He headed to the best place in town to get a home-cooked meal and smiled when he saw Melissa's car out front.

It was only a day before their next date, and he'd been trying to think of a million excuses to drive by her new place. He'd even bought her a bottle of Champagne but had been too busy to swing by and drop it off, so he'd decided to keep it for their picnic instead.

He walked into Mama's and realized that he hadn't been there since it had been remodeled after the tornado. When the bell chimed on the door above his head, several guests stopped talking and glanced towards the door to see who had walked in, one of them being Jamella, Mama herself.

The woman hadn't changed in all the years he'd known her. She wore the same teal outfit and white apron as she had always. Her hair was still short and hung in soft curls around her face and she was still as large as life.

"Who dat?" she asked as she handed a pitcher of water to the patron she'd been serving. "Is dat my boy?" She walked over, her eyes squinting as she looked him up and down. "I heard you was back in town." She stopped right in front of him, her hands poised on her large hips. "But then I thought, no way dat boy would have come up here and not seen his mama before too long."

He glanced at his feet. "Sorry, I've been kinda busy."

"Yes, sir, I heard dat too. Being thrown off a horse and landing on your head." She made a tsking sound and shook her head. "Boy, I thought you known'd better den dat."

He laughed and looked at her. "Are you going to give me a tongue lashing all day, or do I get a hug?"

He watched her face melt into a smile. "Fine, but next time you come here first."

"There won't be a next time. I'm fixin' to stay."

"Ohhh, weeeee. Dat does deserve a hug." She clapped and when he felt her arms wrap around him, he knew he was home.

CHAPTER 5

"You did what?" Melissa sat across from Reece and frowned at him.

"I made an offer on the Jones's place."

"Howard and Barbara Jones's place on Old Airport Road?"

He nodded, and she couldn't help it, she started laughing.

"What?" he asked, now frowning.

"Oh, that's just rich," she said between laughs.

"What?" he asked again, looking at her like she was crazy.

"Nothing." She shook her head and tried to stop laughing.

"Missy, if you don't tell me what's wrong with the Jones's place right this instant—"

"What?" She stopped laughing, then leaned forward and whispered. "You'll spank me?" The beer she'd had after dinner had relaxed her enough that she was coming out of her shell.

His frown fell away as she saw his eyes heat.

"You're asking for it," he said in a low voice, and she felt a shiver run up the back of her spine. Her smile froze on her lips as she leaned back and watched him, her entire body heating under his gaze. Someone's laughter in the crowded room broke the spell and she shook her head.

"Missy?" She tilted her head. "I like that. No one's ever called me that before."

"It suits you." He smiled and leaned back in the booth. She nodded. "Are you going to tell me what's wrong with the Jones place?" He crossed his arms over his chest and stared at her. Before she could answer, Jamella walked over and sat a huge plate of food in front of him.

"Thanks." He smiled up at her. "I've been looking forward to your fried chicken since the last time I was here."

She smiled and patted her hair. "Well, if'n you need more…"

He nodded as she filled up his iced tea.

After Jamella walked away, he turned to Missy without touching his food. "Well?"

She smiled. "There is nothing wrong with the Jones's place other than the fact that it backs up to the Douglas's place, which is the main reason the Joneses left in the first place."

He frowned at her and picked up a piece of his chicken. "Douglas?" She watched him sink his teeth into the tender meat. She'd finished her plate of the golden goodness less than five minutes before he walked into the diner, yet her mouth still watered at the sight.

She nodded. "John and Ruth Douglas and more important, their daughter…"—she paused for effect—"Savannah."

He chuckled. "Is she really as bad as everyone says?"

Melissa nodded. "Worse, I'm sure. Actually, she's been banned from Mama's after a rather suspicious dine-and-dash incident." She leaned forward and whispered, "I've heard that the sheriff was called."

"No," he whispered back as he smiled. She nodded and took another sip of her warm beer.

He watched her, then nodded towards the almost empty glass and asked, "How many of those have you had?"

She shrugged. "One, but tomorrow is my day off and after spending all day yesterday moving, and then pulling a double shift, I needed it."

She leaned back and drank the rest of the golden liquid. "Besides, I live just two blocks from here now and can easily walk home."

He nodded. "Just the same, I'll walk you there once I'm done with dinner." He shoveled a big spoonful of mashed potatoes into his mouth. She watched as his eyes rolled and then closed on a moan. "I don't know how she does it, but these are the best mashed potatoes in the world."

"Garlic and lots of butter," she said, smiling. When he looked up at her, she shrugged her shoulders. "I asked her once. When will you know if the Joneses accepted your offer?"

"Sometime next week. I think the place is just right for me."

"Oh?" She looked down at the empty glass and wondered if she could handle another beer.

"Sure. The barn looks like it had some work done on it

recently. Mike seemed to recall them putting a new metal roof on it just a few years back. It looks like it's in great condition. There are several corrals that will work perfectly for what I have in mind, and there are plenty of green fields for horses."

She giggled and when he looked up from his food, she continued, "Did you even look at the house?"

He replied with a shrug.

"I mean; you do plan on living there. Right?"

"Sure, I guess." He frowned as he took a bite of a sweet roll.

"If I remember it right, it's a brick ranch." When he nodded, she continued. "I think I spent the night there once when their daughter Jenny and I were friendly in grade school. I believe there is an old stone fireplace in the middle and the rooms are near the back." He nodded again and continued to eat. "I remember the kitchen the most. Mrs. Jones baked the best carrot cake. Jenny and I would sit at the stone bar and wait for the buzzer on the stove." She closed her eyes and remembered the richness that had melted in her mouth.

When she opened her eyes, she motioned for Jamella to come over.

"Jamella, do you have any carrot cake?"

She laughed. "No, honey, but Willard did bake up a batch of brownies. I can get you a piece."

She nodded her head and vowed to learn how to make carrot cake in her new place.

"That sounds good. Bring me a piece, too," Reece said, setting his empty plate aside.

After eating their brownies, they walked towards her new place. The streetlights had come on and hummed overhead. Almost everyone in town was at home or in the diner, so the streets were dark and quiet.

Half a block down, he reached out and took her hand in his. She felt his warmth spread up her arm and throughout her entire body. It had been too long since she'd felt this way about someone.

"Did you get all settled in your new place?" he asked when they reached the first corner.

"Yes. It's a very small place, but I like that it's within walking distance to the clinic."

"It was quite a shock about the sheriff and Jamella, huh?"

She laughed. "And they weren't the only ones with a secret. I remember when Lauren and Chase sprung it on everyone that they'd been married for seven years."

He laughed. "Yeah, that even surprised us."

They stopped in front of her new place, and she looked at the front porch. "It's really a cute place, isn't it?"

He turned and looked at the small green classically styled house. "It looks like something out of a fairy tale. You know you expect Little Red Riding Hood to come bouncing out with her basket of goodies."

She laughed. "There are a few homes like that in town. I've always liked this one and the one just around the corner that looks like Hansel and Gretel would chow down on it."

He laughed and she turned towards him. "You really didn't look at the Jones's home?"

He shrugged. "If I don't like it, I figure I can fix it up. Maybe even tear it down and rebuild, if it came to it."

She shook her head. "I suppose that's the difference between men and women." His eyebrows shot up in question. "I wouldn't rent this place until I saw the inside. The outside is cute, but until I walked inside, I wouldn't have lived here for free if the Sheriff had told me I could." They stopped on the lit porch and she reached in her jean pockets for her keys. "Would you like to come in for some coffee?"

He thought about it for a moment and then shook his head no. "I'd better not."

"Oh?" She frowned.

His fingers pulled her chin up until she looked into his eyes. "There is nothing that I'd like to do more than to come inside, but I think you and I have different ideas as to how the night should end, and I don't think you're ready for that...yet."

She thought about it and nodded slowly.

"But I have no objections to sitting on that swing with you for a while." He nodded towards the front porch swing and she smiled.

Reece tried to keep his mind off the images he'd conjured up of them together. Something had stopped him from taking her up on her offer to go inside. He knew that if he walked through the door of the little place that he wouldn't walk out until sunrise.

He didn't know if it was the respect he felt for her or the fact that everyone in town would have known that he stayed the night. He didn't care what others thought of him, but he did care what they thought of her. She had been a respected member of the town for her entire life. Hell, her parents lived just a few blocks away.

"You're awfully quiet," she said, sending the swing rocking again.

He looked down at her and smiled. "I was just thinking about our picnic tomorrow. They say we might get some spring rain, but I'm sure it'll be clear for our ride."

"Oh," she frowned a little.

"What? You're not thinking of backing out, are you?"

"Of course not." She quickly turned her head towards him and gave him a defiant look.

"Good, because I have it all planned."

"I was just wondering where I put my boots."

He laughed. "If you can't find any, I'm sure my cousins have a few pairs lying around that ought to fit you." He glanced down at her feet. She was wearing a pair of black and white sandals that sparkled brightly in the light of the front porch. Her toenails were painted a deep red, making him think of a very juicy apple. He wondered if they tasted as good as they looked.

"What?" She glanced down at her toes with a frown on her face.

He shook his head clear and decided it was high time he headed home since he couldn't keep his mind clear. "I like your toes." He chuckled and started to get up from the swing, but before he could, she leaned closer and wrapped an arm around him, holding him still.

"You know, I had hoped to sit on my sofa and neck for a while, but I guess the front porch will have to do." She leaned in closer and gently put her warm lips on his.

All thoughts of going home cleared from his mind. His fingers tightened, and he gripped the bottom of her shirt. Relaxing his hands, he pushed them up until he touched her shoulders and pulled her closer to him. Her mouth wouldn't stop moving over his, and her tongue rubbed against his erotically, causing his mind to be lost in the moment.

She moaned. He moaned. Her hands had moved up to grip his hair in an almost painful fashion, but now they were starting to roam over his shoulders and chest.

His fingers dug into her hips, crushing her to his side. When he felt her move against him, he gasped for breath and pushed her back. He couldn't explain it, but he felt like he had to take it slow with her. He wanted too.

It was hell, but he finally pulled back from her. He waited until she blinked a few times and looked into his eyes.

"I'd better be going." He brushed a finger down her cheek to feel the softness of her. Her blue eyes were foggy, and he knew without a doubt that he was doing the right thing by taking it slow.

She nodded and leaned back. "I'll see you tomorrow. Around ten?" He nodded. She turned towards the front steps but then turned back towards him. "Listen, I don't want you to get the wrong impression."

His eyebrows shot up.

"You know." She crossed her arms over her chest, but then quickly uncrossed them and started pacing the small porch. "About me. I mean, that I'm…" She turned and looked at him. "You know."

He shook his head no. "No, sorry." Then he chuckled. "I have no clue what you're talking about."

"About us. This." She motioned to the front swing. "I'm not the kind of woman who jumps into bed with anyone," she finally said, causing him to almost burst with laughter.

"Of course, you're not. If you were, I'd have no problem carrying you over that threshold, and I wouldn't give a damn who knew that I'd spent the night in your bed." He walked up to her, placing his hands on her shoulders. "Like I said, my mother died when we were young, but she did teach us a few things before going."

She nodded and smiled a little. "I'll see you tomorrow then."

He nodded and then placed a soft kiss on those rosy lips of hers one last time.

CHAPTER 6

"Just because I haven't ridden in a while doesn't mean you have to take it easy on me." She glanced over at Reece, who was on a dark horse next to her. Since leaving the barn almost a half an hour ago, they had crossed the field at a slow pace. So slow that she was beginning to wonder if the mare she was on could go any faster.

"I don't know what you're talking about." He looked over at her with a smile. She tried to ignore the skip in her heartbeat when he looked at her like that, but the truth was, that smile set off too many sparks in her body to ignore.

"We can go faster." She hadn't wanted to take off and leave him behind, but now she was thinking it would be a great idea to leave him eating her dust.

When he glanced over at her with a smile, she nudged her horse into a trot. When she noticed that he was right beside her, she pushed the horse faster until they were rushing across the field. The wind blew her hat onto her back, and she felt it pulling at her hair. Laughing, she stole a glance sideways to see if Reece was beside her. He was, and his eyes were fixed on her, a large smile on his face as he steadied his horse into position right next to her.

She took that as a challenge and nudged her horse faster. They raced until they came to a small stream that crossed the field. Here there were trees and brush that would shelter them from the warm spring sun. Pulling her horse to a stop, she wasn't surprised to see Reece stop right beside her.

"That was fun." He had a mischievous look on his face.

"What are you up to?" she asked right before he moved his horse right next to hers and plucked her off the saddle. She landed in his lap with a gasp, which he covered up with his mouth on hers.

She'd dreamed about this last night after he'd left her hot and wanting. She hadn't been able to think straight, and it had taken her almost two hours to finally fall asleep. Then the dreams had started and no matter what she did, Reece had always been there.

"There," he said, pulling back from her. "That's better." She shook her head and smiled. "What do you say to some food? I don't know about you, but I'm starving." He helped her down and then dismounted from the horse himself. She followed him when he took the reins and tied the horses to a low branch of a tree near the water, allowing them to drink from the stream.

He took a large picnic bag from his saddle, spread out a large checkered blanket, and then started pulling plates and food from the bag.

"There are some cold drinks in my cooler bag." He

nodded to his horse. She walked over and untied a large brown bag. When she unzipped the lid, she realized it was full of ice. Sitting on the blanket next to him, she reached in and pulled out a couple of bottles of water. Twisting the cap off, she took a sip. Ever since his kiss, she'd felt overheated. She reached in the bag again and took out a bottle of champagne.

"I got that to celebrate your new home." He nodded towards the bottle. "I meant to take it by your place the other day," he said, holding up two champagne glasses. When she took them from him, she realized they were plastic and smiled. He'd thought of everything.

They sat and ate their lunch together in the shadow of a large mossy tree, listening to the water run over the small pebbles in the stream. After she'd eaten half of her turkey sandwich and drank most of her glass of champagne, she leaned back and looked at him.

"How's the leg?"

He chuckled and shrugged. "It's okay. Still on duty?" His eyebrows arched in question.

She shook her head. "Just curious. I'm sure you're used to it…all the bumps and bruises."

He shrugged again. "It comes with its perks." He looked up at her through his lashes and she felt her face heat, his meaning made clear by the look he was giving her.

"Still, you really should take better care of yourself." She looked off across the field and sighed. "It's been too long since I've been riding. I've missed it."

"You look like you're a natural at it."

"Oh, I was taught by one of the best riders. Your cousin." She smiled. "Haley made sure to teach all her friends. I remember when Haley, Holly, and I decided to take Dash, Fresco, and Bob—"

Reece interrupted with a burst of laughter.

"Alex's horse." She rolled her eyes and continued with her story. "We decided to take the horses on one of our first outings. I think we were thirteen. It was before Haley's father passed away." She shook her head. "Anyway, Haley had decided that we'd spend the weekend up at their old cabin." She leaned back on the blanket after taking the last bite of her sandwich. "We were about halfway up the hills when Bob was spooked by a snake and threw Holly. She landed square in the middle of a big pile of blackberry bushes. It took me almost an hour to clean up all the cuts on her arms. It's one of the reasons I decided to become a nurse. That and the time I had my tonsils out."

He leaned back next to her.

"So, what about you?" When he glanced at her questioningly, she continued. "Why did you choose to work with horses?"

He smiled. "They were the only thing in my life that didn't talk back or hit." He crossed his arms behind his head and rested back. "The first time my father put me on the back of a green bronc, an unbroken horse, it threw me clear across the corral. Broke both bones in my wrist." He held up his left hand and turned it several times. "My father cussed and yelled at me and swore that he'd never let me on another horse since I cost him two hundred bucks at the ER. Wore the cast for about a week, then sawed it off myself and crawled back on that horse till he stopped foaming and bucking." He laughed. "When he finally settled down underneath me, that was the moment I knew what I wanted to do for the rest of my life."

She reached over and took his hand in hers. They were both lying on the blanket, staring up at the leaves in the tree above them, which blew in the breeze.

"How did you get into bronc riding?"

He turned over onto his side, resting his head in his hand as he leaned up on his elbow.

"After my father died, I had a pile of bills to pay." He shrugged a little. "It was the only other thing I was good at which I could make enough money to help pay the bills."

"Do you enjoy it?" She leaned over and mimicked his position.

"Busting?" She nodded. "Sure, but it doesn't match the thrill of having that connection with a wild horse for the first time." He reached out and brushed a strand of hair away from her face. "Knowing that your training will carry with them for the rest of their lives…how much enjoyment they'll have by connecting with their rider…"

She smiled and leaned down to place a kiss on his mouth. "You're pretty amazing."

He chuckled. "Not really."

She shook her head. "It takes a certain kind of man to do what you do. You've been hurt doing it but you still climb back in the saddle and love it." She shook her head, then gently cupped his face and kissed him again. This time she put more emotion into her lips. When she pulled back, her heart was racing.

She looked down into his green eyes and could see the desire in them. "Why don't we pick up where we left off last night? After all, there are no neighbors to gossip or see what we're doing today."

This time the kiss had more power as his hands wrapped around her waist, and he pulled her down on top of him. It excited her to feel the hardness of his chest against hers, to run her hands up and down his muscular arms as his tongue played over hers. She used her hips and ground herself against him until she heard him moan and reverse their positions. Now she was pinned under his weight and enjoying the feeling of him hovering above her. His hands shook as they reached up and started unbuttoning her blouse.

She was thankful that it was still early enough in spring to avoid the sheen of sweat that one usually got by just stepping outside in Texas, but now she felt her body heat just from his touch. She moaned when he finally pushed her shirt wide. He pulled back, his eyes raking over her exposed skin, sending shivers over her body. Finally, she reached up and pulled him back down to her, so she could tug at his shirt buttons. He laughed a little and pulled his shirt off his shoulders. He was wearing a white tank top and when she started tugging on it, he yanked it over his head and tossed it aside.

When he came back down to her this time, it was to skin on skin, and they both moaned with delight. The urgency grew and when she started to tug on his jeans, he pulled back and shook his head no.

"Missy, I'm trying to be good here." He closed his eyes and rested his forehead on hers. "God!" The word escaped him in a whoosh.

"Why?" She wrapped her legs around his hips to hold him closer. "Why not let ourselves enjoy the moment?"

He pulled back and looked down into her eyes. Then he shocked her by sitting up and resting his arms on his bent legs. He looked off towards the water. "It's hard to explain." He shook his head. When she leaned closer to him, he glanced over at her. "It matters." She tried to hide her shock. "You've got to understand." He turned and handed her a shirt. She smiled a little when she realized it was his. She put her arms in the sleeves and held it close to her. He sighed and looked off towards the water again. "Ryan and I had always planned to leave home together. Then he left me there and dad got sick." He looked down at his hands. "After he died, I kind of went a little wild." He turned and looked at her again. "There were a lot of women."

She chuckled. "Reece, I'm no blushing virgin either."

He shook his head. "No, I mean a lot. Buckle bunnies. That's what we called the women who followed the rodeo circuit around. Their sole purpose is to bag a cowboy and well..." He shrugged. "I was one of the easiest around."

She sobered. "Reece, are you trying to tell me something?"

He looked at her for a moment and then laughed. "No, nothing like that. I'm clean. I mean, I've always used protection, and I've been tested every year." He took her hand and raised it to his lips and placed a gentle kiss on her knuckles. "Leave it to a nurse to think that this is physical."

She shrugged. "I guess I can understand."

"I guess I used them to fill the hole in my life. I was lonely and thought that sex would fill the void. Coming back here"—he pulled her close, tucking her close to his side— "and making the commitment to stay, I guess I decided I wanted something more. A real relationship."

She pulled back a little, so she could look up at him. "Isn't that what we have?"

His eyes smiled, but there was still a frown on his lips. "Is it?"

When she nodded, he leaned down and placed a soft kiss on her lips. "Good, then you understand?"

She nodded and gripped his shoulders. "Now, can we pick up where we left off?"

He chuckled. "Far be it from me to leave a woman in need."

Reece knew what he wanted and where he wanted it, and contrary to Missy's plans, it wasn't going to take place in a field in the heat of the day. So instead of taking his own pleasures, he set out to make sure she could take her own.

Pulling his shirt gently off her shoulders, he marveled in the beauty of her pale skin in the sunlight. The leaves overhead shadowed them, causing the daylight to play over their skin. He used his mouth and hands until he felt her moan under his fingertips.

When he started tugging on her tight jeans, he took a moment to appreciate how well they fit. "Thank god for Levi's. The man should have earned a Nobel Prize for keeping women in tight jeans."

She chuckled and sat up to help him tug the denim down her legs. He helped her pull her riding boots off, and when she moved to take his off, he quickly discarded them, making sure to be careful around his ankle.

"Does it bother you that much?"

He looked over at her. "No. I was supposed to have the

screws removed a while back, but just haven't had time to do it."

"Oh, you know—" He put a finger over her lips.

"No shop talk. Not now." She smiled, and then she shocked him by taking his finger into her mouth and sucking on it until he felt his eyes cross. She was making it hard not to think about his own pleasures when her sweet mouth worked on his digit so skillfully.

Pushing her back gently, he decided two could play at that game. He ran his tongue down the side of her neck and down the outside of her rib cage until he landed on her soft belly. Using his fingers on her hips, he moved her legs wide until she lay open for his exploration.

She was wearing pink cotton panties with a matching bra and he realized that he had never found cotton so sexy before. When he touched her above the cotton, she squirmed and moaned. Then he moved the cotton aside and set his mouth to where his fingers had just been, and she gasped.

She tasted better than the champagne, and he knew he'd quickly become addicted to her. When she reached down and tugged on his hair, trying to pull him up to her, he chuckled.

"No, let me just enjoy you." He leaned back towards her but stopped. "Tell me what you want, what you need."

He watched her sink her teeth into her bottom lip. "You."

He chuckled and shook his head. "No, specifics." He leaned closer. "Like, do you like it when I do this?" He ran a finger over her pink skin and watched her eyes close. She nodded her head, keeping her eyes shut tight. "Tell me. Just tell me what to do."

"Touch me," she said, and he chuckled again.

"And?"

"Put your mouth on me."

"Like this?" He leaned down and placed his mouth to her again, kissing her lips until he felt her move with his movements.

"Yes, now use your tongue," she gasped.

He did as she asked and was happily surprised when she exploded in his mouth.

"Perfect," he said against her skin and realized that he'd never meant something more in his life than that.

CHAPTER 7

Melissa was finding it hard to concentrate. It had been almost a week since she'd gone with Reece on the picnic, and she hadn't been able to get her mind off of what had happened since. The day had been filled with much more than just heat. They had talked and laughed together during their long ride. After lunch, they had slowly made their way back to the barn and hadn't arrived until shortly after dark. She'd never enjoyed a man's company more than she had that day.

Every second that she found a moment to be alone, she thought of him. Of their conversation, of what he'd done to her. Of what she wanted him to do to her the next time they were alone. She thought of a million reasons to call him or to text him. She had hoped that he would contact her first, but as soon as she got off work, she was heading over to his place at Saddleback Ranch. Just as soon as she ran home, showered, and put on something sexy. Maybe even see-through. That would teach him to ignore her for six days.

When she stepped outside after her shift, she noticed that the streetlights had already come on, and the sky was filled with wonderful hues of pink and orange.

As she began to walk, her mind was consumed with different scenarios. She would show up at his door with a trench coat on and black silk stockings and undies underneath. Or she would wear a very short skirt and a low-neck shirt with heeled boots. She smiled at the images her mind conjured up.

She was so deep in her thoughts about how to seduce him that she almost walked right past him. He was reclining on the front porch swing, his booted feet crossed at the ankles as he rested back against the soft pillows she had bought just two days before.

When she stopped at her front door, keys poised and ready to unlock it, he slowly untangled himself and stood up. He started walking towards her without saying a word and for a moment, another scenario popped into her head. One of him pushing her inside, then against the back of the door, ripping her scrubs off her body and taking her right there.

She felt her knees go weak at the thought.

"Hi," he said in a low voice, stepping closer to her.

"Hi." She couldn't think of anything else to say. So instead, she attacked him. Well, to be fair, they kind of both fell on each other. Her back was pushed up against the door, the door handle poking into her left butt cheek. She had enough wits to fumble with her keys and unlock the door. They both almost fell in when she twisted the knob and the door swung open quickly.

He laughed a little and stepped back, raking his hands through his hair. She'd left the hallway light on and could see the layer of dust that covered him. His shirt and jeans were covered in mud and grime. She could tell that he'd had a long hard day and realized that he had never looked as sexy as he did now.

"You look like you've had a rough day." She leaned against the door.

He nodded. "So, do you." He nodded to the spot of blood on her scrubs.

"Comes with the job." She nodded towards some blood on his shirtsleeve. "Looks like you've scraped yourself up again."

He lifted the arm and looked at the nasty scratch going down to his wrist.

"Comes with the job." He smiled. "I probably smell like the bad end of a horse." He stepped back with a frown. "But I wanted to see you."

She smiled. "I probably smell like baby vomit. I'm glad you came by."

He nodded and just looked at her. "Did I ever mention how sexy you look in your scrubs?"

She laughed. "Even covered in vomit and blood?"

He nodded.

"I think you look sexy all dusty and covered in mud." She walked over to him and took his hat from his hands, then set it on the table by the door.

"This may be a little forward of me, but how about a shower?"

He smiled. "I like the way you think." He walked towards her and she tugged her shirt over her head and tossed it on the ground. She smiled when she saw his eyes heat.

"I've been thinking about getting naked with you all

day." She walked over and yanked his shirt open, sending buttons flying in every direction. They bounced and scattered all over the hardwood floor. He smiled and shook his head.

"You're in trouble now." He took her mouth and started to push her up against the wall.

"Mmmm, no. Shower first." She pulled him towards the back hallway where the master bedroom held some of the best secrets of the small house.

When they walked into the bathroom that consumed the entire back wall, he laughed. "It's bigger than the living room."

"The sheriff claims he started to remodel it a few years back and went crazy." She walked backward and smiled at him. "There's a Jacuzzi tub and the shower has thirteen shower heads."

He moaned. "Bathroom of my dreams."

She laughed. "That's what I said when I saw it. One of the reasons I signed a six-month lease."

She stripped off her pants and watched as he started to unbuckle his belt. When he sat down on the edge of the tub to remove his boots, she toed off her tennis shoes and wiggled her toes. It felt good since she'd been on her feet for almost nine hours.

Then her mouth went dry as he started to slide his worn jeans down his narrow hips. His thigh muscles were bigger than she remembered. He was tall and lean but still built like a boxer. Every muscle in his body was toned to perfection. She couldn't stop herself from staring at him as he stood in front of her with nothing but a pair of boxers on.

"Well?" he asked, chuckling a little.

"Hmmm?" She couldn't take her eyes off him.

"Missy," he said, chuckling, "if you keep looking at me like that, this won't last very long."

She blinked a few times and realized she was almost drooling. Walking slowly towards him, she reached around for the snap of her bra, only to have him shake his head.

"No, let me." He took a step towards her. "You make simple cotton look sexy as hell." Then he reached for her and she started to shake. As his fingers lightly ran over her cotton bra, she was mesmerized by the fire in his eyes.

"Reece," she whispered, not wanting to break the spell he had her in.

"Easy." He used his hand on her lower back to bring her a step closer to him. When she felt his heated skin next to hers, she almost came undone. No man had ever made her feel so alive before, not by simply touching her.

Finally, he leaned down and placed a soft kiss on her lips, melting her even farther. She wrapped her arms around his shoulders as he unfastened her bra. She watched his eyes as he looked at her.

When she reached for his boxers, he held still, and she could tell he was holding his breath in anticipation.

He was beautiful. Her eyes roamed over his naked body in wonder. Then he was tugging down her cotton panties and they were racing again. They walked backward a few steps towards the large glass shower.

"How do you turn this thing on?" he said after a minute of turning knobs.

She chuckled and reached over to turn the right one, making sure to set the temperature to something that wouldn't cool off the mood. "Here." She pushed a button, turning on all the shower heads.

"Mmmm." He leaned into the spray and wrapped his arms around her, holding her tight. "We may never leave this room." She rubbed her hands over his chest as he claimed her mouth again. When he pushed her up against the cool tile walls, she moaned and took everything he offered.

His fingers gripped her hips as he turned her around. She held onto the tile walls as he ran his hands over her back until finally, he reached lower to the place where she ached. Closing her eyes, she rested her head against the wall and held on until her toes curled.

"Tell me you want more," he whispered into her ear. "Tell me you want me," he said as he slipped on a condom.

"Yes," she nodded, blindly. "More. Please. I need you."

She gasped when he slipped into her. She felt her inner muscles scream with pleasure as he flexed inside her. Then he was slowly moving behind her as she gripped the walls. "Faster," she moaned. "More."

He leaned forward and placed a kiss on her shoulder, then gripped her hips and did as she asked.

"More," she moaned over and over, tossing her head back and forth. She didn't even know what she was asking for. All she knew was that she needed all of him.

He lengthened his strokes, went deeper, and still, she craved him. Then he leaned closer, his slick skin against hers and placed a fingertip on her clitoris, and she exploded around him.

"My turn." He chuckled and turned her around. He helped her place one leg up on the long tile bench along the back shower wall and spread her legs wide, holding onto her so she wouldn't slip and fall. "Hang onto me, baby." His fingers tightened on her thighs as he slid once more into her.

Her shoulders were up against the tile as the water massaged their bodies. She opened her eyes and blinked some water out and focused on his face. His green eyes were bright as he watched her face. He was building her up again and she found it utterly fascinating that she could recover that quickly. Throwing her head back, she succumbed to her desires and convulsed around him once more.

Her arms went lax on his shoulders, her knees and legs felt like rubber, yet he still held her up, pinned against the tile walls, one leg still on the seat, one barely touching the ground as he pounded in and out relentlessly.

"Please," she asked when she felt herself building.

He laughed, actually laughed at her, causing her eyes to open. "I told you, you were in trouble." He smiled, then leaned down and claimed her mouth in a kiss that had her climbing faster than before.

"Come with me," she begged, feeling herself about to slip.

"Mine," he growled out finally as she convulsed a third time.

Reece's ears were buzzing. His hands and feet felt numb and even his heart betrayed him by skipping a few beats.

"Damn," he said, still keeping his eyes closed.

Missy chuckled. The rich sound vibrated in the tile shower. The warm water still hit him in the middle of the back, both of his thighs, and several other spots that felt too good for him to want to move just yet.

"I've really got to install one of these in my new place."

She pulled back quickly, almost causing him to slip on the wet tile.

"You're new…Did you get the Jones's place?"

He nodded, and a smile crossed her face. "Well, congratulations are in order."

"I thought that's what we were just doing." He smiled.

She playfully pushed him on the shoulder. "Here, we need some soap." She grabbed a handful of creamy liquid from a rather large bottle and began scrubbing her wet hair.

The smell of her soap was intoxicating. He took over for her and started to rub the bubbles in her long honey hair. She turned away from him and leaned her head back, enjoying his touch. He ran his eyes over her and couldn't help but smile. She was so different than any other woman he'd ever been with. He'd never showered with anyone before, never gone on a picnic, or even spent the whole night with someone else.

He'd never thought to do those things before. Until now. When she turned around and started rubbing the soap over him, his thoughts came back to being with her right now.

When they stepped out of the shower and dried off, he wondered how he'd convince her to allow him to spend the night. She'd pulled on a pair of tight gray cotton pants and a red University of Texas shirt, making him remember who he was with and the lines that separated them. She was an educated woman who had spent years becoming a nurse.

He had barely graduated high school and had gone on to ride in the rodeo. The plans he'd been dreaming about in his head came to an abrupt halt.

"Have you had dinner?" she asked him after he'd pulled on his shirt and jeans.

He looked over and shook his head no. "I was working on fixing the corral, so I can start busting tomorrow."

"So soon?" She frowned a little.

He smiled. "I did get clearance from my doctor. Even if the nurse doesn't agree with him."

She pouted a little and crossed her arms over her chest. "I still think you could use another week." He shrugged and reached for his boots.

"What do you say to some food?" She walked over and took his hands before he could put his boots back on.

"Sure, I guess I could eat," he said, casually trying to hide the fact that his stomach had been growling before their shower.

"Great. I've got a new recipe that I've been dying to try out."

"Are you a good cook?" he asked, following her into the small kitchen.

"I won't burn it if that's what you're worried about." She smiled at him, looking over her shoulder. She took two bottles of cold beer from the fridge and popped the top on one and handed it to him. "Sit. Drink. Watch." She nodded towards a bar stool.

"I could help." He took a large drink from the bottle and smiled.

"No, I got this. Sit." She smiled as she put on a Texas star apron and got to work.

She moved around the small kitchen with quick and

fluid motions. She was as efficient as a chef as she was as a nurse. No motion was wasted. Soon the small place smelled wonderful, and he felt his stomach begin to growl even more.

"I can set the table," he said, taking the dishes and silverware from her.

"Okay, have at it." She leaned up and placed a kiss on his cheek.

When they finally sat down at the table to a large spread of garlic chicken, spiced rice, mixed veggies, and a pan of cornbread, he realized it was the first time a woman had cooked him a meal. He was happily surprised to find that the food was as good as what you get at Mama's.

Over dinner, they chatted about his plans for his new place.

When both of their plates were empty, she took his hand and whispered, "Stay the night."

And for the first time in his life, he knew exactly what he wanted.

CHAPTER 8

Reece was covered in sweat. That night, he'd received the worst beating his father had ever delivered. Blood had dripped from his nose and lip, and he had avoided looking at himself in the mirror for fear of passing out. he had no idea what he'd done to set his father off. Other than existing.

Ryan typically avoided the worst of their father's wrath, but this time, his brother had stepped in and taken a worse beating than he had.

They had talked about ganging up on the old man once, but fear had overridden their plans. Their father wasn't beyond taking a belt to them the next time if they stood up for themselves, even if they were sixteen.

Now, his entire body shivered as he heard his father return home. After the beating, he'd jumped in his beat-up truck and driven into town, no doubt heading to Ray's Bar to drink away his guilt. Both boys knew that it didn't mean the beating was over and feared for his final return that night.

When the truck door slammed shut, both boys jumped in their beds.

"Do you think he'll come in?" he asked Ryan.

"I don't know. Shhh," he said, as they listened to their father struggle to open the front door.

Reece lay there breathing hard and listening to his father stumble around the house. When their bedroom door opened, it was dead quiet. He felt his heart skip as his father sat on Ryan's bed.

He waited with his eyes squeezed shut for the sound of his father yelling or the crack of his hand on Ryan's flesh, but instead, he heard his father start to cry. He peeked his eye open and watched his father lift Ryan from his bed and hug him.

"I'm sorry, boy," he cried over and over again. Even then, Reece didn't chance moving. He knew that the bond between his brother and his father was different than the one he and his father shared. While his father might apologize to Ryan, he had no doubt that he'd turn around and slap him.

So, he lay there in his bed and listened to his father apologize to his brother for the beating they had both received, and when their bedroom door shut, he cried himself to sleep silently.

"Reece?" Someone was shaking him. "Are you okay?" He reached out and took the comfort that was given to him, wrapping his arms around Missy and pulling her close. "It's okay," she kept saying in his ear. "I'm here."

He must have fallen back to sleep holding her. When he woke again, her hair was smothering him. He brushed it aside and looked over at her. She was beautiful in the early morning light. Her hair was tangled and a mess, but it still smelled wonderful from their shower. When he ran his hand over it, it was silky smooth. He felt her stir in his arms and smiled when her blue eyes opened.

"Good morning," she said, leaning up and placing a kiss on his lips. His heated blood began to boil.

"Yes, it is." He reversed their positions until he was looking down at her. Now her hair was fanned out over the white pillow; her smile grew, and her eyes sparkled.

He leaned down and took her mouth again and wondered if he'd ever tire of the feel and taste of her. When he slipped into her, she moaned and wrapped her legs around him, pulling him closer.

They made love slowly as the sun heated the room and then enjoyed showering each other once again in the large shower. She grabbed a clean pair of scrubs and tied her hair up and looked as fresh as could be as she toasted him some bread and chatted about her plans for the day. He sat there in his dusty jeans and shirt, thinking about how his first horse was arriving in less than an hour. He couldn't explain the excitement that ran through his veins.

"You didn't hear a word I said, did you?" She smiled across the table at him.

"Hmm?" He looked at her, his mind snapping to attention. "I'm sorry." He shook his head.

She laughed. "It's okay. I'm sure you're totally pumped for today." She shook her head. "It takes a strong man to be a cowboy, but busters are a different breed." She reached over and took his hand. "Just don't let me catch you visiting the clinic again." She squinted until he finally answered with a "Yes, ma'am."

When they stepped out on the front porch, he was happy to note that there wasn't a soul around. Hopefully, he could walk her to the clinic and get back to his truck, which he'd parked half a block from her place last night, without anyone seeing them together. He really did care what people thought of her. He didn't want the whole town talking about them.

They were half a block from the clinic when he spotted the sheriff's truck around the corner near the diner. He groaned inwardly and held onto Missy's hand tighter.

"What?" She stopped talking about horses and glanced at him. When he nodded to the sheriff, who was now slowing down and rolling his window down to talk to them, she smiled.

"Did you really think it would remain a secret?"

"I had hoped," he said right before the sheriff called out.

"Morning, you two." He stopped his truck right in front of them. "Lovely morning for a walk." The old man didn't miss a beat. Reece saw him notice his day-old clothes and he knew without a doubt that Stephen Miller was no fool.

"Morning, Sheriff. They say we're supposed to get a spring storm in the next few days. We have to enjoy the blue skies while we can," Missy said. Her smile was extra bright this morning.

"I'd heard you were back in town, Reece. Also heard you made a bid for the Jones's place."

"Yes, sir. I'll be closing the end of next week."

"That soon?" The sheriff pushed his Stetson farther back on his head. "Whew. They sure do move things fast nowadays."

He nodded. "The place has sat empty for over a year."

"Has it been that long?" He smiled. "I can hardly

believe how time flies. It was just yesterday I was picking Melissa here up off the road after she'd scraped her knees running too fast."

Reece saw the look the sheriff gave him and got the man's meaning clear enough. He was treading on thin ice and the good sheriff wanted to make it clear that he was watching out for her.

He nodded since no other words were needed.

"Well, I'll let you two kids get back on your way. Melissa, tell your folks Jamella and I would love to come to dinner this weekend."

"Will do." Melissa smiled and waved as the sheriff drove off. "Whew. I think you got off easy." She turned and wrapped her arms around his neck.

He laughed. "Considering the man carries more ammo than most Texans, I guess you could say that."

"So…" She looked up at him through her eyelashes. "What do you say to dinner this Friday?"

He smiled and pulled her close. "Your place or mine?"

"I was thinking my folks' place."

He stiffened and frowned. "Your parents?"

"Sure, it's a standing offer every Friday night. I think Grant and Alex are coming with the baby this weekend."

"Well, I don't…"

"Don't go turning skittish on me now. If you can stare down a mean bronc, then you can have one dinner with my family."

"And the sheriff," he added.

She laughed. "Yes, and the sheriff. And don't forget Jamella."

He shivered. "I don't know who's worse…"—he took her hand and started walking towards the front door of the clinic— "your dad, your brother, the sheriff, or Jamella." He turned to her and placed a kiss on her nose. He smiled when she laughed.

Melissa was in over her head. She knew she needed to call for backup, but she didn't dare waste the time. It had been two days since Reece had stopped by her place and they'd spent what she was starting to think of as the best night of her existence.

Now she was down on her hands and knees and wishing she had a man around more permanently. She tossed her gloves down and glared at the betrayal that was her new yard.

When she'd moved in, the grass had been green, and all of the flowers had been in early spring bloom. Now, however, the grass was quickly turning brown and most of the flower bushes were black and shriveled up. How was it that she could keep a human alive with no issues, but she took one look at anything green and it shriveled up and died on her?

She leaned back and felt like throwing the little spade she'd bought at the local hardware store across the yard. "Ugh!" she screamed. "I can do this." She got up and dusted off her shorts.

"Problems?"

She turned to see Holly standing at the back gate, her arms crossed over her chest. She was wearing a pair of bright pink running shorts and a black tank top with pinstripes down the side. Even her running shoes matched the outfit. Her long red hair was tied up in a ponytail.

"No." She turned and glared at her yard. "Yes." She threw the spade down on the brown ground. "I can't seem to get anything to grow."

Holly chuckled. "I know it might be obvious, but have you tried watering?" Holly asked, opening the gate and stepping into the terror that was Melissa's backyard.

"Of course, I've watered it. The sprinklers are set to go off every night." She motioned towards the small box at the back of the house.

"Let's have a look." Holly walked over and opened the box and then turned back to her and laughed. "These are set to go off once a week." She turned a knob and made a tsking noise. "It was set to winter mode. In this spring heat they'll need to go off at least every other day and, by the looks of it"—she glanced back at the brown yard— "every night might be even better." She punched some buttons and the sprinklers started spraying water over the crisp yard.

"I don't know how you do it." She stood next to her friend and frowned. "You know something about everything."

Holly turned to her and laughed. "It helps when you're stuck inside a bookstore, eight hours a day, five days a week."

Melissa shrugged. "Still."

They moved aside and stood on the wide back deck when the sprinklers turned their way.

"I was just jogging by and heard you scream." Her friend sat in one of the deck chairs.

"Want some tea?" Melissa opened the back sliding door.

"I'd love some. I'm trying to keep my New Year's resolution by jogging every week."

Melissa took the tea out of the fridge and grabbed two glasses. "How's that going?"

Holly rolled her eyes. "It would be better if it wasn't getting so hot." Her friend took a large drink of the tea. "And if I didn't have treats in my store every day." She leaned forward and whispered, "Got any treats?"

Melissa chuckled. "I was going to make some lunch after I had fixed my flowers." She looked at her yard, which was still getting soaked by the sprinklers. "But, since you helped, I think I owe you more than lunch."

Holly leaned back. "More is good." She took a sip of her tea.

"I've been wanting to make some carrot cake. I got a new recipe online." She stood up, and Holly followed her into the house.

"This is such a cute place," her friend said, sitting at the little bar area. "There's one major problem with living in the same building you work in." Her friend frowned. "You can never get away."

"You could always find another apartment," she said, taking out her recipe and gathering the items she would need.

"You know…" Holly leaned her elbows on the countertop and watched her. "I've been thinking about moving everything."

Melissa almost dropped the eggs as she spun around and looked at her friend. "You mean, out of town?"

"Oh, god, no." Holly sat back up. "I'm not crazy. I love Fairplay. It's where I want to get married, raise a family, and grow old." She smiled. "I'm talking about finding another building downtown that could house what I have in mind. Something I can expand to a small coffee shop. Mama's is a great diner, but I think Fairplay could stand a more upscale sort of thing. A place not only to get books but someplace they could come and sit down and read those books and enjoy. You know, a place to get away for a while. Maybe even have wine in the afternoons."

Melissa thought about it. "Holly's Coffeehouse and Wine Bar?"

"Sure, I like the sound of that. But, it will remain a bookstore at heart."

"Holly's Bookstore, Coffeehouse, and Wine Bar." She smiled when Holly laughed. "Are you sure you're not taking on too much?"

Holly snickered. "What else is there in my life, right now? It's not like I have a tall, handsome, cowboy knocking down my door. Like you." She added after a moment of silence.

Melissa turned and smiled at her. "He is handsome." Her friend leaned forward again.

"So, spill. I want to know all the details. Don't leave anything out."

When Melissa just looked at her, Holly shrugged her shoulders. "What? If roles were reversed, you'd be knocking down my door, wanting to know everything. Besides, it's been almost a year since I went out on a date."

"A year?" Melissa was shocked.

Holly shrugged her shoulders again. "It's hard to find a good man in a town of three thousand."

She turned to her friend. "Maybe we can do something about that."

CHAPTER 9

*R*eece stood in the corner and tried to act like he fit in. Hell, to look at him, he did fit in. Every man in the place was cut from the same mold. They all had on crisp Levi's, boots that had been spit-shined, and cotton button-up shirts that had been either starched or ironed. To top off the appearance, every man in the dim place wore a ten-gallon hat on his head.

The difference was, everyone else was having a grand ol' time, while Reece stood in the back and tried to be invisible. He hated bars, always had. Maybe it had something to do with the fact that nothing good had ever come out of his father visiting one. Maybe it was the fact that he'd avoided them while on the circuit. Whatever the matter, he wondered why he'd allowed Haley and Alex to talk him into coming that night.

Thursday nights were karaoke nights at the Rusty Rail and they both had promised he'd have fun. They'd strong-armed him into going and supporting them while they each got up on stage and sang.

Alex and Haley were swaying on the dance floor with their husbands. They had all been chatting at the small round table he stood behind until a slow song started floating through the speakers. Then they had disappeared on him, leaving him alone in the darkened corner. He didn't mind, actually; he was wishing he'd thought to call Melissa and invite her along, but it had had been so last minute, he hadn't had time.

He was taking another swig of beer when he watched the two girls walk in the front door. They looked like they were inseparable. Their arms were linked, and they were laughing as they scanned the room.

When Missy's eyes locked with his, her smile brightened even more. She nodded and said something to Holly who immediately looked over towards his corner with a large smile on her face.

They started walking his way, and his night instantly got better.

"Fancy meeting you here," Holly said, walking over and sitting on one of the bar stools. She looked at her friend and nodded. "I ran into Melissa earlier, and we decided a night out was in order."

He nodded and pulled Missy closer to him. "I'm here with them." He nodded to his cousins who were now dancing faster on the old wood floor with their husbands.

"They look good together," Holly said. He thought he heard a hint of jealousy in her voice, but he didn't know her well enough to tell.

"You clean up well," Missy said.

He smiled. "So, do you." He leaned down and kissed the red lips he'd been staring at since she walked in the door. She was wearing a flowered cotton sundress covered with little red roses. Her red boots matched her lips and the little red purse she had strapped over her shoulder. He couldn't stop touching her.

"I'll go grab us a pitcher," Holly said, quickly retreating towards the bar.

"I'm glad you came," he said, running his hands up and down her back.

"Me, too. Holly stopped by and we got to talking, and then we decided to come here and try to find her a man." He chuckled.

"Her? Not you?" He smiled.

She shook her head. "I've already got a good man."

He nodded. "I don't suppose you'd like to dance with your man?" He nodded to where his cousins and a half-a-dozen couples were swaying around the dance floor.

"I'd love to." She took his hand and followed him to the floor.

When they began to slowly move around, using the moves most Texan's are raised from birth to know, he smiled at her. "You know; I normally wouldn't be caught dead in a bar."

Her eyebrows shot up. "Oh?"

Nodding, he continued. "I never could stand them. Crowded, loud, smoky."

"Fairplay has been smoking free for three years." She nodded towards the dark room. He could tell. When he'd walked in, it was the first thing he'd noticed.

"I like it. My father smoked. Never could stand the smell."

"Oh, I don't know. My father and uncle smoke cigars on special occasions. I'm quite taken with the smell of those." Her arms felt good wrapped around him. Pulling her closer, he felt her heart skip a beat next to his.

"So, tell me what your friend is looking for in a man," he asked playfully.

"Why?" She laughed. "Know anyone in particular?"

He thought about it. "Local?" When she nodded, he thought harder. "Can't think of anyone."

"That's the problem around here. Good men are hard to come by."

"Oh?" he said, twirling them towards a dark corner. "Is that why you were so eager to go out with me?'

She laughed. "Point taken. I was a fool."

Just looking at her smile made him smile. He stole that moment and leaned down to place a kiss on her lips.

"Are we still set for tomorrow night?" she asked when he pulled away and they started walking back towards the table. He didn't know why he was trying to avoid dinner with her parents. He'd met them at Alex's wedding and they had seemed very nice. Hell, he'd probably run into them in town several times since coming into town. It wasn't as if they were mean people. Actually, that's one of the reasons he had wanted to settle down in Fairplay in the first place. There wasn't one person in town he could think of that he didn't like.

"Yeah. I'll pick you up at seven?"

She nodded and smiled at the group sitting around the table.

"Look who I found." He pulled Missy closer to his side, showing everyone his interest in her.

"It's good you guys came alone. We were getting tired of trying to convince Reece to look like he was having a good time," Alex said as she playfully punched her cousin's arm.

"Well, I hope you don't mind, but I'm gonna have to steal one of your men soon. I'm wearing my dancing boots and I'm desperate," Holly said, swaying to the song that was playing.

"Take mine," Haley said, holding her sides. "Since having the twins, I need to sit down every other song."

Wes leaned down and kissed his wife's cheek then held out his arm for Holly. "I'm all yours, for now."

"He won't admit it, but he loves to dance," Haley said watching Wes and Holly swing across the floor.

"Look who's back in town," Alex said, nodding towards the bar. "I heard she was in Houston getting another boob job."

Reece almost choked on the sip of beer he'd just taken.

"Sorry," Alex cringed.

He shook his head to let her know it was okay. He'd never had sisters around, but he knew how open his cousins were.

When he finally got around to glancing towards the bar, he was surprised to see Savannah standing at the bar, staring at the group. When she noticed him looking at her, she smiled and stuck her chest out a little farther.

He remembered their run-in at the Grocery Stop the week he'd arrived in town. His eyes dropped to his beer and he tried not to look her way again, as the group continued to talk about her.

"I heard it was a nose job this time," Haley whispered.

"No, she had one of those when she turned eighteen." Alex waved her sister off. "But there is something different about her."

"Maybe she was visiting Travis. Wherever he disappeared to," Haley suggested. "Well, whatever the reason for her almost month-long disappearance, she's back in town and our problem now."

"Is she really that bad?" he asked, taking another sip of his beer.

"Worse," Alex said, glaring towards the bar. "I guess in a way I have her to thank for my marriage, though." His cousin blinked a few times and her eyes softened as she looked over at her husband.

At that moment, Reece realized that his strongest desire was for someone to look at him just like that. At least once in his life.

"Can you believe our luck?" Holly said, leaning against the porcelain sink. Melissa was reapplying her red lipstick, which she was very happy Holly had talked her into wearing that night.

"What do you mean?"

"I mean, it's wonderful that Reece was here." She nudged her. "By the way, Haley and Wes agreed to take me home tonight." Holly winked at her, and she couldn't help smiling.

"You're a dork."

"Yes, sadly, I'm a dork that will be going back to an empty apartment." She faked a frown and gave her sad eyes, blinking a few times.

"There are plenty of good-looking men out there." She nodded towards the bathroom door.

Holly laughed. "Right."

"What about…" Melissa tried to think of a few guys they had gone to school with that were still single.

"Ha! Can't think of any, can you?" Her friend pointed at her.

"Joey."

"Joey? Joey Briggs?" Holly held her arms out and made her face chubby.

"Okay, so he's gained a few pounds since school."

"Ha, he's no quarterback anymore, that's for sure." Her friend teetered on the sink and Melissa reached out to steady her.

"Maybe you should see about having Haley and Wes take you home soon."

Her friend waved her aside. "I'm not toast yet."

Melissa laughed and helped her off the sink just as Savannah walked in.

"Well, well. Look who got lucky."

If Savannah's dress were any tighter, Melissa was sure it would have broken several laws of physics. Her breasts did look bigger and she wondered if what Alex had said was true.

"Hello, Savannah." Melissa turned towards the other woman, still holding Holly steady. Now her friend was leaning a little more on her shoulder.

"Wow, how big can they get?" Holly asked, earning her a pinch on the arm from Melissa.

Savannah gave Holly a look that said everything. It was obvious that Holly didn't even warrant a response from her.

"Well, Melissa, it's very lucky for you that I had to leave for a very important meeting for daddy's business in New York."

Savannah crossed her arms over her chest and continued to block the only exit from the small room.

"Oh? Why is that?" she asked, taking the bait. She knew better, but for some reason, she was dying to know what Savannah was up to.

"Well, before I had to leave, Reece and I had started something that would have, no doubt, ended up being much more than what you have." She smiled and looked down at her perfectly manicured fingernails. "But I'm sure it won't be long before he becomes bored with you." She sighed and looked up at her, her eyes raking over her simple cotton dress. Then she chuckled. "I'll be sure to have him tested, first."

It happened so fast, Melissa didn't have time to respond. Holly wiggled out of her grip and before Melissa knew what was happening, there was blood splattered over the three of them.

When it was over, Holly stood over the crumpled and much larger Savannah. Savannah had fallen to her knees and was holding a very broken nose in both of her hands, screaming at the top of her lungs.

"Don't ever talk like that about someone I love." Holly shook her fists. "Everyone in town knows that the only one carrying any STDs in this town is you. Besides, you couldn't get a hold of a good man like Reece. Even if you roped and hog-tied him. Everyone knows that all you care about is stealing everyone else's men."

When Holly finally stepped back and Melissa could see the actual damaged her friend's tiny fists had done, her nursing instincts kicked in. She may be small, standing at only five-three, but Holly Bridles could punch like a pro boxer. It was rumored that her father had been quite the pro back in his Navy days.

Melissa would have laughed, except for the amount of blood that was streaming from Savannah's face. Then the bathroom door swung open and Carl, one of the bouncers for the Rusty Rail, rushed in demanding to know what had happened.

By then, Melissa had a clean towel covering Savannah's nose as the woman continued to scream. Holly stood with her back against the wall, staring at the scene with a frown on her face.

Savannah's friends rushed into the bathroom and gathered her up so they could drive her to the clinic, while Carl grabbed her and Holly by the arms and rushed them to the manager's office. Reece and Melissa's brother were right behind them, followed by everyone else from their table.

"What's going on here?" Reece demanded.

"I'm holding these two until the sheriff gets here," Carl said, motioning for them to sit on the sofa in the manager's office.

"That doesn't answer his question." Her brother crossed his arms over his chest.

"One of these two broke Savannah's nose in the lady's restroom. I'm too busy right now, so I'll leave it up to the sheriff to get more details from them," he said, as he picked up the phone and dialed.

Reece looked at her, and she saw his face pale. Then she noticed everyone else was looking at her too. Glancing down, she realized why they would think she had punched Savannah. Her dress was completely covered in Savannah's blood. She looked up and shook her head and then looked over at Holly, who had her arms crossed over her chest and a determined look on her face.

"Go, girl!" Alex chimed in, only to be nudged by Haley and Wes.

"Reece?" She started to worry that he might pass out, but he was avoiding looking at her skirt and had taken a seat on the edge of the desk. She stayed where she was and tried to cover up as much of the blood as she could with her arms.

Less than a half an hour later, everyone was crowded into the small sheriff's office a few blocks away.

"Why does it seem that trouble seems to follow you Wests?" he asked, sitting behind his desk. When everyone started talking at once, he held up his hand and picked up his ringing phone.

"Yo," he said. "Yeah, so I hear. Are you sure?" He looked towards Holly and frowned. "Right. Okay."

When he hung up, Grant stepped in front of Holly. "As Miss Bridles' attorney, I'd like to know the charges."

The sheriff laughed. "There won't be any."

"What?" Everyone looked over at Holly, who had stood up, her hands on her hips.

"That was John T. Douglas, Savannah's father. It seems that Savannah slipped on a broken tile in the women's restroom at the Rusty Rail and fell face first into the sinks. I've been telling them for years to fix those floors." The sheriff shook his head.

"That's a lie." Holly stepped forward, only to be grabbed and hushed by Grant. "But it's wrong. They're going to sue the Rusty Rail."

"It doesn't matter. I'll represent the bar," Grant said, trying to hold the hundred-pound woman back.

"Grant," Holly began.

"Wes, Haley? Would you two make sure Holly gets home okay?" Grant nodded towards them.

"I'll make sure she's okay." Melissa stepped forward. "After all, we went together tonight."

Melissa gathered her friend and was grateful when Reece followed them outside.

"I'll drive," he said, taking Holly's other arm. Even then, Holly was trying to get back to the sheriff to explain. She kept saying, "It's not right."

When they all got into Reece's truck, Holly finally settled down, and they drove to the bookstore in silence.

"Do you think they'll win?" she finally asked when they'd parked in front of the small store. "The Douglas's?"

"I'm sure the bar has sufficient insurance to protect against situations like this," Reece said.

"I'd just die if they had to close down on account of me," Holly said, sniffling a little.

"Holly." Melissa waited until her friend looked at her. "My brother and father are damn good lawyers. Neither one of them are going to let any Douglas get their hands on another piece of this town, least of all shut down a major hub that provides the people of Fairplay the only entertainment we have."

Holly looked at her nodded. "You're right. I'm sorry I ruined everyone's night."

Melissa laughed. "Are you kidding? That was the most fun I've had since…well, forever." She reached over and hugged her friend. "Remind me to bring you along the next time I'm trying to give a five-year-old his shots."

Holly laughed, and Melissa jumped down from Reece's truck so Holly could scoot out of the middle seat.

She hugged her friend again. "Thanks for sticking up for me."

"Don't let Savannah get to you. You have a good man there." She nodded towards the truck where Reece was sitting behind the wheel, waiting. "Have a wonderful time and stop by later this weekend to tell me all." Her friend reached up and kissed her cheek.

Melissa stood on the sidewalk and watched her race up the outside steps towards the apartment that sat over the bookstore.

"That's some woman," Reece said when she got back in the truck.

"Tell me about it. I've never seen a man punch that hard, let alone a five-foot fairy princess."

Reece laughed. "That description suits her."

She smiled. "I'll make sure to never piss her off." They both laughed.

CHAPTER 10

It wasn't until he pulled up in front of Missy's place that he felt the nerves kick in again. He knew what he wanted but wasn't sure she was going to invite him in again.

He glanced over at her and saw that her pretty dress was ruined, covered in dried blood. Now that it was a darker red, he didn't feel the wave of dizziness come over him like he had in the sheriff's office. She probably wants a shower and her bed, he thought.

She turned in her seat and looked over at him. "Well, are you going to come in or do I have promise you some carrot cake and coffee?" She smiled.

He laughed. "I was just trying to figure a way in the door. But carrot cake does sound good." He reached over and pulled her across the front seat of his truck. Then he was kissing her, and all his nerves fell away.

"I may need another shower," she said, pulling back and looking down at her dress. "Not to mention a new dress."

"It's a shame too. I really liked this one." He got out and pulled her out his side of the truck, helping her down.

"Yeah, but I bet I didn't spend as much on this dress as Savannah spent on her outfit tonight."

He chuckled as they walked through her front door. He followed her back towards the kitchen where she pulled a large pan from the refrigerator. "How big of a piece would you like?" She took down two plates and turned to him.

"You made it?" he asked.

"Yes, my first attempt. Holly said it was so good, she wants me to make some for her shop next week."

There were two pieces cut out of the cake already; it looked so good that his mouth started watering.

"I'll get this. Why don't you go change out of that dress?" He nodded to her ruined outfit.

"Oh, I'd almost forgotten. You did wonderfully in the sheriff's office earlier." She set the plates down and turned to go. "There's milk in the fridge. For some reason carrot cake and milk go hand in hand."

By the time he had cut two pieces of cake and poured two glasses of milk, she'd walked back into the room. Her hair was wet and she was wearing tight tan yoga pants with a white tank top. His mouth watered for a second time since walking through her door.

"So, Savannah said that you two had something going," she said while taking a nibble on her cake.

He almost choked on the piece of cake he'd shoved into his mouth. When he finally could breathe again, he realized she was smiling.

"Don't worry, your secret is safe with me."

"God." He took a drink of milk to help swallow the

knot that was in his throat. "It's not like that." Words just wouldn't come to him. "Really."

She just chuckled and took another bite of her cake.

"I ran into her at the Grocery Stop. That was it. Nothing else happened. I swear, Missy."

"Reece." She waited until he looked into her eyes. "You don't have to explain anything to me. We both came into this knowing each other's pasts. Besides, I trust you."

He was floored. He could see in her eyes that she did trust him, and that was something he hadn't had in a long time. Since his brother had been around.

"Is that what the problem was tonight?" he asked, cutting himself another piece of cake.

"Sort of." She leaned back and looked at her empty plate. "She said things. I said things. Then Holly clocked her." She chuckled.

"Well, I'm sorry if I was the cause of it."

"No, Savannah was just being Savannah." She picked up her plate and walked it to the sink and then leaned back against the countertop. He left his second piece of cake untouched and wrapped his arms around her waist. She felt so good.

"I'm glad you showed up tonight." He leaned down and placed a kiss on her lips.

"Mmmm, me too." She wrapped her arms around his shoulders. When the kiss heated, he hoisted her up onto the countertop as her legs wrapped around him.

His hands snaked under the cotton tank top and just the feel of her silky soft skin had him moaning with delight. He pressed up against her core and moved gently, giving her pleasure.

When he pulled the tank top from her, she arched back,

giving him full access to her exposed skin. He lapped up every inch, enjoying the fact that her nipples puckered for his view. When he returned to her lips, she started unbuttoning his cotton shirt and then pulled it from his shoulders. When she slowly dragged her nails across his skin, he almost lost it. He started yanking on the yoga pants and cursed them when they were hard to get off her.

She giggled and helped. "I love how tight these are on, but they do take some work to get on and off." She tossed them aside and his mouth went dry. She was sitting on her countertop completely naked, and he realized he has starved again.

She reached over and undid his belt buckle, pulled his belt off, and started tugging at his jeans. He didn't want to waste time yanking off his dress boots, so instead, he moved back between her legs and took her mouth in a heated kiss.

She responded with a moan as he ran his hands over every inch of her. When she rubbed her chest over his bare skin, he lost all control and plunged into her right there as she sat on the kitchen counter.

Melissa didn't want to move. Yet the cold tile of the countertop was making it hard to get comfortable.

"I'll move in a minute," she heard him say against her neck.

She chuckled. "S'okay." Her head rested against his shoulder, where she'd placed it after having one of the best orgasms she'd ever experienced. "I kinda like it right here."

"If my jeans weren't around my ankles, I'd carry you into the bedroom."

She laughed again.

"What?" He leaned his head to the side to look over at her.

She shook her head. "I can just imagine how we look right now."

He chuckled and rested his head back against her skin. "Don't get me started again." His voice was husky, causing a wave of heat to travel throughout her body. Her legs were still thrown around his hips and he was still inside her. She tested the waters and moved just an inch and felt him respond, so she moved again.

"Missy," he warned.

"Hmmm?" She ignored him and moved again.

"I had hoped to have the second round in the comfort of your bed," he said against her skin, and then he nibbled his way up to her ear, causing goosebumps to rise all over her body.

She arched back, giving him access. Her fingers gripped his thick hair as she moaned and enjoyed what his mouth was doing to her.

"Yes," she said, holding him close. "I love the feel of your mouth on me."

His hips rocked slightly as he began to move in her again. Her legs automatically wrapped around his hips, pulling him as close as she could.

Their hearts beat against one another, and moans turned into cries as the excitement escalated. Finally, she felt herself falling just as he cried her name.

"I need another shower." She giggled as he stepped back and handed her the clothes off the floor.

"How about I join you." He looked over his shoulder. "Then maybe we can have some more of that cake as we watch a movie."

She smiled and nodded. "Sounds like a plan."

When they had finally settled down in the bedroom for the night, her flat-screen television playing an old John Wayne movie, she felt like she could finally relax.

Less than an hour later, she was woken by Reece twitching. He'd woken her like this the first night he'd stayed at her place. Now, however, he started talking as well. She listened to him beg his father to stop hitting him and when she couldn't stand it any longer, she reached over and gently woke him, then snuggled down against his chest when he pulled her close like he had done that first night.

The tears silently leaked from her eyes as she lay there unable to sleep, worried about the little boy who had to beg to not be hit.

The next morning, she woke early and decided to try one of the cinnamon roll recipes that Holly had given her. She tried to keep the noise to a minimum, but baking was a messy and loud experience for her. When Reece walked into the kitchen, looking damn sexy in just his boxers, she almost dropped the pan of rolls she'd just pulled from the oven.

"Something smells good in here." He walked over and waited until she set the hot pan on the counter, then leaned in for a kiss that had her wishing she'd stayed in bed with him. "Mmmm, someone tastes good, too."

She smiled. "Well, every good chef knows you have to taste your food. I just need to ice these. I've also made ham and cheese omelets."

"Wow," he said, looking at the spread she had laid out for them. "What have I done to deserve all this?" He smiled.

She reached up on her toes and kissed him, feeling her heart bind a little. "You don't need to do anything to deserve this. Just be who you are."

When they sat at the table, she watched him dig into his omelet while her food sat in front of her, almost forgotten.

"Reece, you told me your father was hard on you." She twisted her hands under the table.

He looked up at her and frowned a little, and then he nodded. "Yeah, he was a hard man to get along with." He shrugged his shoulders and went back to eating. "But Ryan and I dealt with it."

"But you still have nightmares about it." She waited and saw the weariness creep into his eyes.

"Yeah." He set his fork down. "I've never stopped having them. Ryan used to quiet me before I woke our father. I'm sorry if I woke you." He reached over and took her hand.

She shook her head. "It's not a problem. I was just worried." She squeezed his hand.

He looked across the table at her. "You know; I've never talked to someone else about it before. Other than my brother."

"I'm here if you ever want to talk about it."

"It's kind of weird. Saying it out loud doesn't take away any of the hurt, but somehow it makes me feel better. Not that I want pity." He looked at her. "But I don't see pity in your eyes."

She prayed that the tears that had been building up behind her eyes stayed there. "No?"

He shook his head. "No, I see something else."

"If I didn't already know that your father was dead, I'd send Holly after him."

He laughed. "I'm not sure my old man could have handled a spitfire like her." They laughed.

CHAPTER 11

When Reece arrived at Missy's door the next evening to pick her up, his palms were sweaty, and he couldn't stop the butterflies in his stomach from jumping. When he'd been getting dressed for the dinner with Missy's parents, he'd realized with a jolt that it was the first dinner he'd ever gone to like this.

Then she opened the door and his nerves fell away. She was worth all of the discomforts he would feel during the evening. The simple gray dress hugged the curves that he loved. Her sand-colored hair was tied back, accenting the beauty of her face. Her blue eyes sparkled as she looked at him.

"Well, don't you look handsome?" She gasped happily when he pulled the small bouquet of flowers out from around his back.

"Your beauty outshines these by far." He smiled when she looked at him.

"Oh." She smiled and buried her face in them, then reached across the doorway and pulled him in for a kiss.

"I'll just go put these in some water, and then we can walk over."

He nodded and followed her inside. His mind was quickly thinking of a million ways to convince her to stay and let him peel that dress off her, but he knew that none of them were good enough. So, he stood in the small hallway and waited for her to come back from the kitchen.

"Ready?" she asked when she came back. He nodded and held out his arm.

They walked the short distance to her parents' house. The sun had yet to set, and the warmth of the day was quickly making his new dress jacket and dark pants uncomfortable.

When they arrived, she pulled open the front door and called out, "Mom, Dad, we're here." He stepped into a house that looked like it had come right off the cover of Better Homes and Gardens. Nothing was out of place in the living room and as they walked towards the voices coming from the back of the house, he noticed how clean everything was.

Missy's place was clean, but it was nothing compared to how her parents' place looked. He preferred the more lived-in look. He was starting to wonder if he would end up embarrassing himself by knocking something over or setting a drink down without using a coaster.

"Back here," someone called out. When they stepped out onto the back patio, he was glad to see that Grant and Alex were already there, along with the sheriff and Jamella.

The Holton's were some of the nicest people in town, but that didn't stop him from worrying. He shook every-one's hands and removed his jacket when Grant offered to hang it up. Instantly he felt the cool breeze hit his shirt and relaxed a little.

By the end of the wonderful meal, he realized he'd been a fool to worry. He'd hadn't attended a family dinner that felt so comfortable since he'd dined at his cousins' place when he'd been a teenager.

They had sat out on the back porch talking and drinking beer until her father was done grilling up the meat. Then they'd gone inside and had eaten at the large table which was made up fancier than any restaurant he'd ever been to. After eating more food than he'd eaten in a long time, they'd all gone back outside and chatted some more. He'd really felt relaxed and at home with everyone.

He'd laughed more that night than he had in years. He listened to stories of Missy and Grant's childhood and wished more than anything that he'd been a part of a family that had actually cared and loved one another.

As he walked her home, he wished more than anything that he could track his brother down.

"You're awful quiet," she said, tugging on his hand.

He shrugged. "I like your family."

She smiled. "I like them, too."

"I wish I could find Ryan," he blurted out and cringed a little.

"Well, have you looked?" She stopped to pull out her keys.

"Yeah, right after he left and again when dad died."

"And?" She opened the door.

"Nothing." He shook his head. "I looked everywhere we'd talked about as children. All the places we'd dreamed of going." He walked in behind her.

"You could hire someone." She laid her purse down and turned towards him.

"Yeah, I suppose. I'd just hoped…" He stopped, not sure what he'd hoped.

"What? That he'd come back?" she asked.

He nodded and realized that the hurt ran deep. "I'm sorry."

She smiled and wrapped her arms around his shoulders. "Don't be. I think I remember meeting you and Ryan once when you guys were staying out at the ranch for a week during summer."

He nodded. "Yeah, I remember."

Her eyebrows shot up. "You remember meeting me?"

He felt his face flush. "Sure." He pulled her closer by using his hands on her hips. "You were going on a ride with Haley. You had on a pink tank-top and faded shorts." He smiled. "They were very short and Ryan and I fought over who was going to ask you out first."

"Why didn't you?" She smiled.

He shrugged. "Dad came and picked us up while you were on your ride."

"That's too bad." She leaned up and whispered against his lips. "I would have picked you." He felt his heart skip as he leaned up and kissed him. She must have felt the urgency in his lips because she moved closer and pushed him back until his shoulders came up against the front door.

He liked letting her take the reins and tried to relax as she rushed to pull and push his dress clothes from him as they stumbled their way back towards the bedroom. When he stood in front of her completely naked, he hiked her dress up with his hands and played with the silky material that covered her. When she moaned and leaned her head against his chest, he walked her towards the bed, falling with her onto the soft mattress, hiking the dress up more.

She was softer than anything he'd ever felt before and smelled and tasted better than anything he'd ever experienced. He wished that the moment could continue forever.

"Reece, please," she begged him. Her head rolled from side to side as she kept her eyes closed tight.

"What Missy?" he asked, knowing full well her answer but wanting to hear her ask him in her sexy voice.

"I need you. I can't stop wanting you." Her eyes opened, and she looked deep into his. "I think about you, day and night. About this. About you." She pulled him back to her lips as he plunged into her, holding her tight.

She was more than he'd ever imagined. The feel of her was intoxicating, the way she consumed his mind, his heart. She made him feel like he belonged. Like he was loved. He stilled when he realized that for the first time in his life, he loved someone completely.

"Reece, please," she called out again, causing him to move. Her nails dug into his hips, forcing his hips to thrust against her. Then his mind shut off as she kissed him, and he let his body take over every movement. His heart rate spiked, his eyesight went dark, even his hearing left him, replaced by a heightened sense of taste, smell, and touch.

The buildup was nothing compared to being with her, inside her. His fingers dug into her soft skin, his lips yearned for hers. Even when he was enjoying her, he wanted more.

He felt her tighten around him just as his body exploded inside hers and he died the sweetest death he'd ever experienced.

❄

Melissa was questioning her sanity. Her breathing had yet to return to normal and her ears were still ringing. But when she played it over in her mind, she could have sworn she'd heard Reece say that he loved her.

He was resting his head on her chest, so she didn't know if his eyes were open or closed. When she heard his heart slow, she thought he was asleep until he leaned up and looked down at her.

"I can hear you thinking," he said, frowning slightly at her.

"Did you mean it?" She scooted back until she leaned against her soft headboard and pulled her skirt back into place. He was completely and gloriously naked and looked very comfortable.

"What?" He moved next to her.

"What you said."

He frowned. "Yeah, but…" She didn't let him get any further as she straddled his hips. She could see the fear in his green eyes and wanted nothing more than to soothe and comfort him.

"I love you, too," she said and watched desire replace the fear. Holding onto him, she gave him a kiss that showed him everything she'd been feeling since he'd first opened those green eyes of his.

When she finally pulled back, she was breathless again and couldn't stop smiling at him.

"What do we do from here?" he asked, rubbing his calloused hands over her skin. She loved the feel of them on her.

"How about a shower?" she asked, causing him to laugh.

That night as they lay tangled together, her mind refused to shut down. She had joked when he asked because she hadn't known the answer to his question. Where did they go from there?

She'd never said those words to a man before. There had been other men in her life, but no other relationship had ever gone this far. They'd eaten dinner at her parents' house, and her parents had pretty much given their blessings.

Of course, in their eyes, no West could ever be bad. But she knew the hell he'd been raised through, and her parents didn't. Still, as she watched him sleep next to her, she doubted he had a mean streak in him. He was not like his father, that was apparent.

She'd seen the tears in his eyes tonight as he talked about finding his brother. She was just drifting off when a memory flashed in her mind. She bolted up and started shaking Reece.

"Reece wake up."

"What?" He bolted up, switched on a light, and looked around. "What's going on?"

"I…I think I know where your brother is."

"What?" he asked, rubbing his hands over his eyes.

"I think I know where Ryan is."

"How?" He frowned, looking at her as he leaned back against the headboard.

"Well, at least I know where he was two years ago."

"What are you talking about?"

"Two years ago I was still interning at the hospital in Houston. That was just after I switched over from Children's. Anyway, one night I was working ER and a man walked in with two bullet wounds to his stomach. He just walked in all by himself. It was amazing he was able to do that. When I reached him to help him to a gurney, he looked up at me and then passed out before I could get his name or what had happened to him. He stayed unconscious while we removed the bullets that were lodged in him. The next day I went to check on him, but he'd been moved to his own room and he was gone. All of us were concerned since we didn't know what had happened to him."

"What has this got to do with my brother?" he asked.

"Well, before he passed out, I remember looking into green eyes." She paused and looked at him. "Your eyes."

"Are you saying my brother is in Houston? And that he was shot two years ago?"

She nodded. "I'm almost certain of it." She thought about it. "I can make a few calls this week and find out if that man ever gave his name or insurance information."

He nodded. "We never talked about going to Houston. There are too many people there. Ryan and I liked country living." He frowned. "Then again, we talked about leaving together."

She moved closer to him and wrapped her arms around him. "It's a lead. Maybe he was just passing through and got mugged?"

She felt him nod. "Did he make it through surgery okay? That man?"

"Yes. The doctors said that he had woken up halfway through it and demanded they leave him alone."

"Leave him alone?" he asked.

"If I remember it correctly, the doctor said that he yelled for them not to touch him." She looked up at him and watched as he paled a little. "Obviously he was well enough to get out of there on his own."

He nodded. "What made you remember this?"

She shrugged. "I'm not sure." Then she remembered the look of fear Reece had in his eyes before she told him she loved him. "I saw something in your eyes tonight that I had seen in his. Identical expressions."

He looked at her, waiting.

"Fear."

CHAPTER 12

The following days were full of paperwork and signing his name. Reece had never bought a house before, but he was sure there wasn't this much paperwork when he'd sold his father's property.

The final inspection and appraisal had been completed and as he sat next to Grant Holton and across from the Jones's, he realized he'd never felt more nervous in his life. How could buying a lot of dirt and a stick of house tie his stomach in knots?

Grant stood up and shook Mr. Jones's hand. "Looks like we have everything finished." Then he turned to Reece and handed him a silver keychain. "The place is all yours."

He took the keys and shook everyone's hands. When he left Grant's office, he wasn't sure what to do next. He'd never owned a place before. Stopping in the middle of the sidewalk, he realized he didn't even have a bed of his own and hadn't owned anything short of a suitcase full of clothes since he'd sold everything after his father had died.

Looking around, he noticed the old antique store that sat across from the clinic. He'd never been in the place and decided it would be a good start. Worse case, he'd buy a used mattress and sleep on it until he could get into Tyler to a furniture store.

Glancing down at his phone, he realized it was just about time for Missy's shift to end. So instead of walking into the antique store, he walked into the clinic instead.

The waiting room was quiet. Only two people sat in the chairs waiting, a mother and a small girl whose pony-tails looked cute enough to tug on. He smiled at them when they looked up at him.

He walked up to the front counter and tapped on the glass. It took almost a minute for the glass door to slide open.

"Yes?" It was a rather large nurse who looked back at him.

"I'm looking for Missy."

"Missy?"

"Melissa Holton."

"Oh." She smiled. "You must be Reece."

Instantly he felt his face flush. So, her coworkers knew about them. He wondered how much she'd told them and all of a sudden, he felt nervous.

"Yes, I thought I'd walk her home after her shift."

"I'll just run back and get her for you. Take a seat." She nodded towards the row of chairs.

When he sat down, he smiled again at the little girl, who had decided not to read the book in her lap but chose instead to watch him. This was one of the main reasons he liked this town—its people. He'd only ever heard of one problem that had bothered the people of Fairplay— and it had involved his family. But good had prevailed and life had picked up after the incident with the previous mayor's wife.

Sure, the town had gone through its ups and downs. There had been not one, but two tornadoes that had ripped through the area in the last fifty years. The first had taken his aunt, a woman he could only remember through pictures and through her daughters' eyes. The second storm had almost taken his cousin Haley in the same way. He shivered when he remembered how close it had come. Then his thoughts turned to Missy. She hadn't been in town for that storm since she'd been away at college, but that didn't stop his mind from twisting and wondering what he would have done had it been her instead.

"Hi," Missy said, standing right in front of him, and he realized he must have gotten lost in his thoughts. "Daydreaming?" She smiled.

He smiled and took her into his arms. "Hi." He brushed his lips over hers. "Are you about done for the day?"

She nodded. "Want to do dinner?"

He smiled. "Maybe after some shopping. I closed today."

"What?" She leaned back and looked at him. "I thought you were closing on Wednesday?"

He laughed. "It is Wednesday."

She stopped and pulled out her phone from her back pocket and frowned down at it. "How did I miss a whole day?" She shook her head and smiled up at him. "Congratulations, homeowner." He enjoyed the kiss and hug she gave him right there in the waiting room.

"Thanks. I was hoping you'd help me out. I need some

items and was going to swing through the antique store across the way."

"Oh, I'd love to. I'm always making excuses to go in there. I just love looking at all the stuff they have. Let me get my stuff and clock out." She kissed him again quickly and rushed towards the back.

He turned and saw the mother and girl smiling up at him.

"Congratulations," the mother said. "I remember when we closed on our place five years ago."

He nodded and sat back down.

"Where did you buy?" she asked after a moment.

"The old Jones place out on Old Airport Road, about five miles out of town."

The woman looked at him and he could see something cross her eyes. "Good luck," she said, just as Haley walked out.

"What kind of items are you looking for?" Melissa asked as they walked across the street holding hands.

He laughed. "Everything."

Two hours later, he sat in an old recliner and listened to his stomach growl. Looking down, he frowned. "I know buddy. Who would have thought that she was a shopaholic?" He laughed when Missy hit him playfully on the shoulder.

"I'm almost done. Besides, we've gotten you some really good pieces." She sat next to him. "What do you say to a home-cooked meal after this?"

"Sounds great." His stomach chose that moment to growl even louder. "When? Where?"

"Mama's, after I finish negotiating for the desk." She

nodded towards the roll-top he'd been eying since walking into the place.

"Fine. Think you can talk him down to two-fifty?"

She smiled. "Just sit back and watch the pro."

Less than half an hour later, they sat in a booth at Mama's and ordered dinner. He'd gotten a great deal on a sofa, a beautiful oak headboard, a matching dresser and nightstand, and the roll top desk he'd been wanting. They would be delivered later that week along with a few other smaller items they had bought.

It was meatloaf night at Mama's and everyone in town knew that Willard the chef cooked the best barbeque meatloaf around. Some said it was a recipe handed down from his family, others claimed it was one he'd made up himself. Whatever the origins, people crowded in when they drove through town and smelled the spices in the breeze.

They'd been lucky to get one of the last booths along the back in the newest section. Shortly after the tornado had gone through town, Jamella had expanded the small diner into what it was today. Now, instead of just a dozen tables, there were over twenty tables and booths. The new tile floors shined. Gone was the old ceiling that occasionally leaked during a heavy rainstorm. There was even a new jukebox in the back that played everyone's favorite music.

The kitchen had been totally remodeled as well, or so everyone had heard. Mama's was the only place in town to get a home-cooked meal and usually you bumped into someone you knew.

Ten minutes after they'd sat down, Holly walked in. She stopped in the doorway and looked around, waving at a few people. Then she spotted Melissa and Reece and rushed over to their table.

"Well, hello. Mind if I join you?" She didn't wait for an answer and instead pushed Melissa lightly until she moved over.

"Sure," Missy said, moving over a little more. "I haven't seen you in a few days."

"I received a shipment of new stock and have been buried in books." She pulled out a book from her rather large bag, which she'd set next to her. "Speaking of which…" She handed it to Melissa.

"Oh! It came." Melissa gripped the book and hugged it to her chest. Then she pulled it back and looked at it, stroked the cover, and smiled. "Look." She turned it around and showed it to him.

All he could tell was that it was a new book. Its cover was bright and colorful.

"Nice," he said, trying not to add too much sarcasm to his voice. Melissa heard it and smirked at him.

"It's Holly's book," she said, looking down at it again.

"Holly?" He looked over at the small redhead, who looked like she was boiling over with joy.

Melissa nodded. "Yes, it's the story of her father's life." She turned and he read the title, *Serving Life*.

"Congratulations," he said, looking closer. "I've never met an author before."

Holly blushed. "It was nothing really. I just took some of my father's journals and an old box of poetry of his and put it all together."

"Whatever," Missy said, playfully pushing her friend. "I know how many hours you put into this. Well, I'm not giving this copy back, and you're going to sign it for me." She hugged it again.

"That's fine. I have a box full of them." She giggled. "I can't believe it."

Just then, the waitress walked over.

"Do you happen to have any champagne?" Reece asked her.

"No, but we do have some sweet white wine." She looked at the three of them.

"We're celebrating Holly's book." Melissa held it up.

"Oh," the waitress said, reaching down and hugging Holly. "Congrats, honey." Then she shocked Reece by putting her fingers to her mouth and whistling. "Listen up, everyone. Holly's new book is here." She took the copy Melissa held up for her and raised it above her head. "I'm sure you can all get your copies first thing in the morning when Holly opens up. She'll probably sign them if you're nice enough." Several people laughed.

Holly stayed and ate dinner with them. Several people stopped off at the booth and congratulated her. Reece really enjoyed watching how she handled everyone and realized he'd yet to make a stop at her bookstore.

It wasn't as if he was a big reader. Growing up the way they had, there hadn't been time for books. Ryan and he had done okay in school, but no one would have called them geniuses. Their father only tolerated them staying in school because it was the law. Once, he'd tried to pull them out for a full semester, but the school had called the truancy officers, and someone had stopped by and set the old man straight.

After listening to Holly talk about some of the times

her father had had during his tour in Vietnam, he began to think it was time he picked up a book again.

When he walked Missy home, he started to follow her in without an invitation.

"Aren't you going to head over to your new place?" She turned and put a hand on his chest, stopping him.

"No." He looked down at her knowing exactly where he wanted to be. With her.

"You have to sleep at your new place the first night."

"Why?" He wrapped his arms around her.

"Well, it's bad luck or something."

He chuckled. "I'd rather be here with you."

"Hmm." She bit her bottom lip, making his mouth water. "There must be a way." She leaned back. "Do you have a sleeping bag?" He nodded, not liking where this was going. "Perfect. I'll just go grab mine and we can swing by and get yours." She stepped away.

"Wait." He took her arm. "You're willing to leave the comfort here and sleep on the floor of a place that probably doesn't have power yet, just in case it's bad luck that I don't spend my first night at my new house?"

She nodded and laughed. "Sounds crazy, but I think we'll have fun. Like camping." She frowned. "My folks never really took us camping. My mother's idea of camping is the Best Western." She chuckled.

"Yet you own a sleeping bag?"

She laughed. "Still in its wrapper." He laughed.

When they finally drove up to his new house, it was after dark. His truck lights lit up the front porch.

"I'd forgotten how cute this place is," Melissa said, leaning forward to get a better look out the window.

He shrugged his shoulders, feeling a sense of pride come over him. This was all his. Sweat and blood. It had cost him more than he'd ever be able to count. He shut off his truck and just looked at it.

"See those lights over there." Melissa pointed off to the left. He could see lights shining through a cluster of tall pines a couple hundred yards from them. "That's the Douglas place." She nodded to the right and he could see more lights about the same distance away. "That's Jamella's place."

"Oh?" He looked closer. "I didn't know she was going to be my neighbor."

"She and the sheriff, now that they're living together." She leaned back and sighed. "This town still has its surprises. Like those two. No one knew that they'd been an item for years."

"Well, are we going to just sit here or are you going to show me in?" She reached around and grabbed her sleeping bag. "I brought you a surprise." She held up a slick black bag.

"What?" he asked, eager to know what was in the bag. He was a sucker for surprises.

"Oh, no. You'll just have to wait until after you give me a tour."

He grabbed his sleeping bag and the large flashlight he'd had enough forethought to grab. When he unlocked the front door, he was rewarded when he flipped the light switch. Lights flooded the front living room.

This space was the one that he liked the least. He had plans to remove the wall between it and the dining room, making the two rooms into one that looked and felt bigger.

"Hmmm, maybe you can take out a wall?" Missy said, setting her sleeping bag down and stepping in.

"I'd thought the same thing. That wall there." He pointed towards the dining room. "There's no need for it." Besides, it was covered in dark wood paneling that had to go.

He started to show her the kitchen but stopped when he noticed a large basket sitting on the bar area. They walked over together. Pulling out the card, he read out loud.

Reece,

Congratulations on your new house. We hope this gift will help turn it into the home of your dreams and make your first night here a little better.

p.s. I took the liberty of having all the utilities switched into your name.

--Alex, Grant, and Laura

"Family. Gotta love them." She smiled at him and gave him a quick hug. "My brother thinks of everything."

He looked into the basket and was happily surprised that there was a bottle of champagne, a plate of Alexis's brownies, a small container of tools, and a roll of toilet paper,

"I just bet the tools are my brother's doing." She smiled. "The toilet paper is Alex's." He laughed because he'd thought the same thing.

They walked around the house, and he showed her around, room by room. They briefly stepped out on the back deck, which he knew needed some work as well. They gazed at the stars and enjoyed the sounds of the crickets and frogs.

"All in all, it's a great place. Could use some new carpet, some paint to update the look." She sighed and leaned against the railing.

He nodded. "It'll do." He reached over and pulled her close. "Now, what did you bring me?" He nodded towards the bag she'd set on the countertop next to the basket. He knew Alex's brownies were good, but he was hoping for something else from Missy.

"You wait here." She reached up and planted a kiss on his lips. "Give me a few minutes and then come on back."

She walked to the countertop, grabbed the bags, then tucked the sleeping bags under her arm and walked towards the master bedroom. Excitement rushed through every pore in his body.

He turned and looked out at his backyard, trying to cool off before he let it get too bad. He knew there was some work out here that needed to be done as well. There were flower beds that needed weeding, some sod that needed replacing, and a few trees needed to be trimmed or chopped down.

He leaned against the railing and imagined what it would look like once everything was done. There would be a porch swing sitting over there, roses along the side, maybe a swing set along the back row.

He shook his head and blinked a few times. Swing set? He felt the blood drain from his face. He'd never thought of having kids before. Never. Actually, when he and Ryan were eleven, they had both decided against ever having kids. They didn't want to end up like their old man.

He turned away from the image of three kids running around the yard, playing on the swings, and walked into the house. Even here, his mind started conjuring up images of kids lying in front of the fireplace, reading or playing games. Of him rocking a little girl with gold locks of hair in a chair as she fell asleep in his arms.

He turned towards the back hallway and blinked. Standing in the hallway was Missy. She wore white and in the dim light, the whiteness of the silk glowed, causing everything else to go fuzzy. The silk flowed as she took a step towards him.

"Reece?" She held out her arms. Her hair was down around her shoulders, looking softer than it had ever before. He watched her breathe, saw her chest rise and fall, and was almost mesmerized by the movements. "Come to bed." She stood there, her arms out, waiting. He couldn't have denied her if he'd tried. His feet moved him forward and without knowing it, he decided his future.

CHAPTER 13

She tried not to let him see that she was shaking when she took his hand and walked back into the bedroom with him. She'd laid out their sleeping bags against the back wall, facing the large window that over-looked the backyard. She'd turned the lights off and had lit the candles in the jars she'd brought along in her bag.

For some reason, she wanted this night to be perfect. Even though they'd been going out for a while, she felt nervous, like it was their first time.

When they walked into the bedroom, he turned her around by touching her hips. His lips curved into a smile.

"Your smell is intoxicating." He stepped towards her.

She put her hand on his chest and felt his heart beat quickly under her fingertips. His eyes heated as she used her fingertips to pull his shirt from his jeans. "Let me." She looked up into his eyes, telling him what she wanted.

He nodded and dropped his hands to his side, and she smiled. She walked around him, slowly running her hands over him, pulling, tugging and unbuttoning, until she heard him groan. "Tell me what you want," she whispered next to his ear, leaning up and nipping at his earlobe. She pulled back when he reached for her and shook her head. "Tell me."

He groaned. "You're killing me."

"Good. Talk to me. It's your turn to talk, Reece."

He closed his eyes and moaned again. "I want you." His green eyes opened and burned into her soul.

"How?" Her mouth had gone dry. "What do you want?" She leaned closer to him. Reaching out, she moved her hand over his bare chest. The hardness of him excited her.

"I want to toss you down on that makeshift bed, hoist your legs above my shoulders, and bury myself deep into your sweet heat," he whispered, and she felt herself grow wetter.

Now her mouth was completely dry. Her mind blank. He stepped closer to her, testing the water. His hand reached out for her, gently taking her hips and backing her up a few steps until she felt the sleeping bags under their feet. Then he leaned close and kissed her, and she felt like she was falling. When her back touched the soft ground, she moaned and arched up into his hands.

How had she lost control this easily? Isn't that what she really wanted? To lose herself in his touch, his mouth, his needs?

He peeled the silk away, and she felt her skin grow hot. She closed her eyes, focusing on every touch, on his sexy musky scent. His fingers dug into her hips as he lapped at her flat stomach, tickling her ribs and sending sparks flying throughout every nerve.

"Reece." She tried to lean up, but he held her still.

"No, your turn." He looked up at her and smiled. "Tell me what you want."

She moaned and leaned her head back. "You. You inside me, consuming me, completing me."

He leaned up and slid slowly into her, placing his lips on hers and catching the moan of delight with his mouth. When he started to move, she locked her legs around his hips and held on. "Yes," she moaned, trying to hold him still, but he chuckled and rolled her over easily.

Then he whispered, "Your turn." When she just looked at him in frustration, he laughed. "Ride me, Missy."

She glared down at him. She'd been on the verge of coming, but now she'd have to build up all over again. Then she started to move and lost complete track of her frustration. He held onto her hips, helping her to move as she pleased them both. When she threw her head back and cried his name, he arched up and took her mouth and followed her.

Later that night she realized that sleeping on a hard floor was a little less glamorous than she'd imagined. Even though the carpet was soft, it didn't cushion her hips our shoulders enough. When she moved for the fifth time in a minute, Reece reached over and pulled her closer.

"Trying to get comfortable?" She nodded, "Missing that bed of yours right about now?"

She closed her eyes and felt his skin up against hers and thought about her soft pillow-top mattress at home and shook her head. "Not if you're not in it with me."

He chuckled. "We could have waited until after they delivered my furniture."

She shook her head again. "It's bad luck."

"Says you." He ran his fingers through her hair and she felt like purring.

"I'm sure it's written down somewhere." His fingers were relaxing her enough that she no longer felt the hardness dig into her hip. His legs wrapped around hers, completing the feel of utter relaxation.

"Missy?" he whispered next to her ear.

"Hmmm?" She couldn't move. Didn't want to move. Didn't want to be anywhere else but here, on the hard floor with him.

"Thanks for coming with me tonight." He brushed her hair aside and kissed her cheek.

"Mmm."

"Night." He rested back as she drifted off.

When she woke a few hours later, she listened to the quiet, unsure what had woken her. Then she felt it; Reece was twitching in a nightmare next to her. Reaching out, she snuggled up to his chest and placed a kiss on his jaw. When she felt him relax again, she smiled and snuggled into his warmth.

The next morning, they showered in the old shower that Reece promised her was the first thing on his list to replace. They drove into town an hour before she was supposed to be at work and parked in Mama's parking lot.

"How about some blueberry pancakes?" he asked looking over at her.

"Sounds great." He helped her out of his truck and she thought that she was finally getting used to a man opening the door for her.

After they sat down and placed their breakfast order, she looked over at him and asked. "So, what's on your list today? More shopping?"

He chuckled. "No, I've got some lumber being delivered today for the corrals I'm building." He looked down at his watch and frowned. "They're supposed to be there around nine." The door chime rang, and Chase, Grant, and Wes walked in. When they spotted Reece and Melissa, they walked over and sat next to them at the table. Chase pulled a chair up from the other table and turned it backward.

"So, you ready to do this?" he asked Reece.

Reece laughed and told Melissa, "I've hired some help."

"Hired? I thought we were doing it for free? But if you want, you can buy me breakfast." He waved the waitress over and the men ordered more pancakes, bacon, and eggs.

By the time the food arrived, the table was the loudest in the room and had enough food to feed an army.

"I wish I could be there to help out today." Melissa frowned down at her almost empty plate, trying to figure out a way to be where all the excitement was going to be.

He reached over and took her hand. "Don't worry about it. It's hot, sweaty work. I was hoping you'd continue to help me inside."

She looked up at him. "What? Like with paint and stuff?"

"Actually, any decorating stuff. I'm no good at it."

"I guess I could help you…"

"Really, other than some of the big stuff, I was hoping you'd kinda take over the whole inside. I'll take care of the outside." He looked at her with pleading eyes.

She laughed and shook her head. "Men. I suppose I could give it a shot." Who was she kidding? She loved to decorate. Where Holly was an expert with clothes, hair, and makeup, Melissa was an expert with décor. Maybe a little of her mother had actually rubbed off on her. Whatever the reason, Melissa loved to put a room together.

During her lunch break, she walked over to the bookstore and grabbed every home décor magazine that Holly had on her shelves. She spent the rest of her break looking through them and coming up with ideas.

After work, she changed into old jeans, stuffed a few things into her duffel bag, and drove out to his place. She parked behind Reece's truck then walked over to the corral they'd built. The men were busy trying to put another post in the ground and didn't even stop when she drove up. She heard them cussing and laughing and turned back to her car to start carrying things inside.

When she walked in, she noticed that the furniture they'd purchased from the antique store had arrived. She spent the next hour arranging it and the smaller items. She made a list of some of the larger items he still needed as well as some basic supplies.

She stood back, a trail of sweat dripping down her back, to look at what she'd done. The living room was still mostly empty, with only a small bookcase and an end table. The bedroom was just missing a few items. The king-sized bed frame needed a mattress. The matching nightstands looked great with the lamps she'd talked him into. The desk had been left in the middle of the floor in the second bedroom. It was too heavy for her to move all by herself, so she left it until Reece could help.

She walked around making lists for each room—what needed to be fixed or replaced, and color ideas from the magazine pages. She hoped Reece would like her ideas and thought of how nice it would be to do something like this for her own place one day. She sighed and leaned against the countertop just as the men crowded into the air-conditioned room.

"Tell me you've stocked the fridge with beer, and I'll forget that you dropped that timber on my foot," Grant said, walking over to the fridge.

"No, sorry…" he started to say and stopped when Grant started pulling out cold beer and tossing them to everyone.

Reece looked over at her and she shrugged her shoulders. "I stopped off and grabbed a few things."

Grant walked over to her and kissed her on the forehead like he'd always done. "Gotta love my sister."

Reece walked up to her and planted a big kiss on her lips. "Yes, yes I do." He smiled down at her.

"If you happen to have a pizza in the oven, I could probably be persuaded to forget the whole hammer incident," Wes said, walking over to the empty oven.

"Nope, sorry." Just then they heard a knock on the door.

"Guaranteed that's the women with food," Chase said as he leaned back against the countertop.

Sure enough, Lauren, Alex, Haley, and Holly walked in carrying large to-go containers from Mama's.

"We decided not to cook tonight," Lauren said handing over a squirming baby to her husband.

Wes walked over and grabbed up one of his sons.

Missy and Holly watched the families and sighed together. When they looked at each other, they giggled a little.

"Do you think they know how cute they all are?" Holly asked, leaning closer to her.

"If not, someone ought to take a picture and show them."

"That's a great idea," Holly said. "Hang on a moment." She rushed from the house. "Here," she said loudly, "everyone get together." The men groaned when they saw her shiny new camera hanging around her neck.

"We've been working outside all day," someone complained.

"And you all look absolutely masculine and damn sexy." Holly smiled and pushed Grant closer to everyone. "Just do this."

Missy laughed when the men all moved closer to one another, carrying their full plates of food with them.

"You too." Holly pushed Melissa towards Reece.

"Oh, no." She tried to walk away. "I've been cleaning for the last hour. I look a mess." She tried to get away.

"That's the charm of it all," Holly said, putting her hands on her hips. "Don't make me get upset. You know what happens if I get mad."

Everyone laughed.

"Holly Hulk," some chimed in.

In the end, Holly won out and everyone, including kids and babies, was shuffled in front of the fireplace for a picture, food and all. She even set her camera on the end table and set the timer for a couple shots.

In several shots, people had full mouths, which only added to the charm of the picture.

"These are great," Lauren said, looking over Holly's shoulder at the screen.

"Thanks. I just got this camera last year and it was my New Year's resolution to start taking more pictures."

"You know; I've been thinking about getting some

family pictures…" She paused when Chase groaned. "Oh, stop your grumbling," she told her husband with a smile. "You look good even covered in dust and dirt." He laughed and went back to shoving food in his face.

"Are you asking me to take your family pictures?"

"Holly's Bookstore, Coffeehouse, Wine Bar, and Photography Studio," Melissa piped in. Holly chuckled.

"What's all that?" Haley asked, rocking one of her sleeping boys.

"Oh, Holly's new idea for the bookstore." She smiled over at her friend.

Holly told everyone her plan for improvements, and they all loved the idea.

"Does Mr. Nolan know your plans?" Grant asked.

"Mr. Nolan?" Alex frowned and looked at her husband.

"Sure, he owns the building." He turned to Holly, who nodded.

"Yes, he's owned the building since before my mother opened the bookstore.

"I didn't know that," Melissa said.

"None of us did, except my husband apparently." Alex looked over at her husband who was holding their sleeping daughter.

"He owns a lot of the empty buildings downtown. When he was mayor, he had big plans to update them. He wanted to see downtown restored to its former glory." He shrugged. "At least that was the plan before…" He looked down at his sleeping girl and frowned. Alex walked over and wrapped her arms around him.

"Don't," she told her husband. "Let's not think about it." Grant looked up at her, nodded his head, and smiled.

"I'm sure I can convince him to let me make the

changes," Holly said. "The last time I talked to him, he was excited about my ideas."

"Well," Lauren said, standing up from the folding chair she'd brought along. "It's past the kid's bedtime."

The cleaned up the plastic plates and put the leftovers into the old fridge.

"Let us know if you need any more help." Grant looked around the place. "There are good bones here. All it needs is some work and some fresh paint."

Melissa and Reece stood on the front porch and watched everyone drive away. When the road was quiet and dark, he wrapped his arms around her and kissed her.

"How was your day?" he asked finally when he pulled back

"Long. But not as long as yours, I bet."

"I hurt in places I'd forgotten I had." He smiled.

"Well, then"—she pulled him closer— "how about a massage?"

"Mmmm, now you're talking." They walked into the house together.

"It'll have to be on the floor since you have no mattress yet."

He groaned. "Okay, first thing tomorrow I'm heading into Tyler to get one."

"Really?" She pulled back. "Because there's a list." She turned to go.

"Go with me." He pulled her back to him.

"To Tyler?" He nodded. "To shop for furniture?" He nodded again. "What about the other items on the list?" She bit her lower lip.

"Whatever." He shrugged.

She smiled and jumped up and down. "I'll call in sick."

CHAPTER 14

The following days were filled with shopping and repeatedly moving heavy things around his house. By Monday morning, his back was sore, and he had a spot on his foot that was numb.

That morning, he had a client delivering a two-year-old quarter horse, the first horse he was going to break in his corrals on his land. He could hardly muster up the excitement that normally came with a new job.

He watched Melissa drive away shortly after downing a breakfast of orange juice and toast. When he walked back into his place, he smiled. He had a leather sectional, coffee tables, and lamps, not to mention the huge flat screen he'd talked himself into at the store, which hung above his mantel. The walls were still bare, but the place was finally coming together. All thanks to Melissa.

He had just changed, making sure he strapped on both knee braces and the back brace he wore when breaking when he heard a car pull up. Walking outside, he was shocked to see Savannah standing on his front porch.

"Well, this is cozy." She looked around at his front porch.

"Hello, Savannah." He stepped out onto the front porch and let the screen door shut behind him. "What can I do for you today?" He noticed that her eyes were still a little puffy from the broken nose, but for the most part, her face was back to normal. She was wearing a tight, tan, low-cut blouse and black leggings that hugged every curve. Her spiky heels made her almost the same height as him.

Her breasts did look a good deal larger, but he didn't think it was his place to stare at them, a fact that didn't go unnoticed by her. She moved closer to him and started rubbing her chest against his.

"Well, I was just stopping by. You know, being friendly to a new neighbor." She purred, running her hands through his hair.

The fact that he'd been there almost a week and she'd shown up the first time he was there alone didn't escape him.

"You know, give you the proper welcome." She placed her red lips on his so quickly he didn't have a chance to pull away.

He was just about to push her away when he heard his client drive up. He groaned inwardly at the timing and then glanced over to see Melissa's car stop at the end of the driveway. She quickly slammed it into reverse and peeled out of the driveway, heading towards town.

Fear shot through him so quickly that he pushed Savannah away and raced towards his truck. He had just made it to the corner when he heard the crash ahead.

❄

Melissa was pissed. How dare he do this to her? She'd given him everything, and he'd barely waited until she'd driven away to get it from Savannah. She should have known that this would happen when he moved in next door to that wench. After all, they'd never really made a commitment towards one another. But they had said they'd love one another.

Could she have misjudged the situation? She blinked back the tears and ran over the scene on the front porch in her mind.

He had looked like he was trying to escape Savannah's grip. Realization hit her like a brick, and she glanced in her mirror so she could pull a U-turn in the road. When she glanced forward again, a huge buck stood in the middle of the road. She jerked the wheel to avoid the massive creature and realized too late that she'd overcorrected. Her car spun and skidded towards the guardrail. She screamed just before everything went black.

When she woke, she heard someone screaming her name. Something was running in her eyes and she blinked to clear them.

"No," Reece said above her. "Don't move. I've called the ambulance." He held her hands away from her face.

"I…I can't see." She tried to blink a few more times but everything looked dark and fuzzy.

"You're bleeding pretty bad, honey. Don't move."

She tried to push him away. "Don't look." She worried that he would pass out and wouldn't be able to stop the bleeding. She tried to get her mind to work, but everything was fuzzy.

"It's okay, I've got you." She heard ripping and then

there was pressure on her forehead and shoulder, and she cried out with pain.

"I'm sorry," he said, soothing her. "I've got to hold this on here hard to stop the bleeding."

"Reece, there's blood," she repeated.

"I know, Missy. I'm okay." He pushed harder on her shoulder. "I wasn't doing anything with Savannah. I didn't even know she was going to kiss me," he explained as he held the compression on her shoulder and forehead.

"I know. I realized that. I know you would never do anything like that." She reached up and touched his face. "That's when I saw the deer."

"Don't move," he repeated, and she could hear the ambulance making its way up the road. "Here comes help."

"I'm sorry," she said, trying to see his green eyes. "I should have known."

"It's not your fault. I should have told you how I felt earlier," he said, leaning his head closer to hers. "It's all my fault."

"How you felt?" Nothing was making sense now and everything was spinning.

He nodded. "I'm more than just in love with you, you know."

Just then she heard tires screech and Tom and Roger, two of the EMTs she'd been working with for the last few months, rushed up and started asking questions.

"Did you get thrown from the car?" Tom asked.

She realized for the first time that she was laying on the hard ground. "No, I crawled out here. I saw smoke." She tried to nod towards her car.

"I put the fire out," Reece said, nodding towards the

fire extinguisher. "I pulled her a few feet more away from the car, just in case."

"Okay," Tom said, getting to work securing her.

When they moved her to the gurney, she realized the extent of her pain. It felt like sharp spikes stuck through both of her legs, and her arms were starting to feel numb. Her head felt light and dizzy.

"Tom, I'm so sorry, I know I'm not supposed to, but I think I'm going to pass out again." Everything turned dark once again.

Reece stood in the waiting room of the clinic, trying not to pace. The small room was crowded, and he felt like there wasn't enough air in there.

"Reece come sit down," Holly suggested, patting the seat next to her.

He shook his head. "When will they tell us something?"

"Soon," Lauren said, holding Chase's hand tighter.

"Why aren't they moving her to the hospital in Tyler? I can drive—" He dropped off as her parents rushed in.

"We just heard." The worried look on their faces almost undid them. When Grant rushed across the room to hug them, he felt a wave of shame hit him full force. This was all his fault. He should have never let Savannah get that close to him. He should have told her he wasn't interested long ago.

Then he realized that her parents were standing in front of him. "You were with her?" they asked. Worry marred their faces.

He shook his head no. "I was following her and heard the crash. There was a deer," He said, feeling like he was about to cry.

When Melissa's mother walked over and engulfed him in a hug, he did cry. Apologizing the entire time, he explained what had happened.

"Oh, you poor dear. Missy, as you call her, is a strong young woman. She knows better than to believe any of that woman's tricks." Carolyn smiled at him. "Besides, everyone in town knows how you two feel about each other."

"I should have—" he started, only to be shushed by her again.

"There's no time for should haves. Here's the doctor now." She stood up.

Dr. Conner held up his hands to stop all the questions. "Melissa is fine. She has a broken collarbone, some bruised ribs, a concussion, and a few new stitches in her scalp and shoulder. We'll be keeping her here for a few days, but she won't need to go to Tyler."

Everyone sighed, and Reece stepped forward. "Can I see her?" The doctor looked him up and down then nodded. "One at a time."

When he walked into her room, her eyes were closed, and he felt like turning and running away. He'd destroyed everything. Here was the only person in his life who had ever loved him, and he'd destroyed it. Destroyed her.

"Hey," she said, her voice weak and low. "Come here."

He looked up to see her blue eyes looking at him. "I thought you were asleep."

She started to shake her head but stopped and groaned.

"No. A concussion means I will be kept awake or checked on for the next twenty-four hours."

"Twenty-four?"

"Yup." She patted the bed beside her. "So why don't you get comfortable?"

He looked around. "Visiting hours are over at eight."

"That's okay. I know a few people, and I'm pretty sure I can convince them that you should stick around. After all, anything to help me heal."

He took a step forward and then another.

"Reece?" she said.

He looked at her, afraid that she was hurting too much. He was ready to run and grab a nurse, when she chuckled, then grabbed her side and sighed.

"I'm okay, really. Come over here."

He walked over and gently sat next to her, taking her hand. She sighed again, and this time he could hear the pleasure in her tone.

"There, much better." She closed her eyes and was quiet. Just when he was concerned that she'd fallen asleep, she said, "Don't leave, okay?"

He nodded then realized her eyes were still closed. "I promise," he said in a shaky voice.

CHAPTER 15

*S*he knew the drill. She had been on the other side many times, but nothing could have prepared her for the pain she felt every time the nurses walked in to check up on her.

The pain of the broken collarbone and the bruised ribs could be managed by a lack of movement, but the concussion hurt every time she opened her eyes. She tried to keep them shut, but the pounding continued in the darkness of her mind. The only thing that seemed to make her feel better was knowing that Reece was sitting next to her.

Her family had come in and visited briefly. Once she'd assured them she was okay, they had let Reece sit beside her.

"He blames himself," her mother told her.

"I know. It was my fault. It was stupid of me to drive away upset." She closed her eyes and thought of how much worse it could have been.

"I would think that the deer would take some of the blame." Her mother squeezed her hand. "Do you know that when your father and I were dating, I hit a buck and totaled my car? The next week I borrowed your father's truck and hit another, destroying his truck as well. I had better luck that year than most hunters." She chuckled with her mother, which caused pain to shoot throughout her body, and when she looked up, she saw a tear escape her mother's eyes.

"Rest. I know Reece is dying to get back by your side. We'll be around." She leaned up and kissed her forehead, and Missy felt better.

"Thanks, Mom."

"You're a very lucky and smart girl. Don't let blame get in the way of what's right in front of you."

When Reece walked back in, she grabbed his hand and held on, knowing that there was a lot she had to say to him once she was feeling better.

An hour later, by the time lunch rolled into her room, she was starving. She started spooning in some soup and nibbling on the bread, but a few minutes later felt dizzy and nauseated.

"Should I call a nurse?" Reece had paled while watching her.

"No." She stopped herself from shaking her head. "It'll pass. It comes with the concussion."

A few minutes of closing her eyes and breathing slowly had helped and allowed her to eat the rest of her lunch.

"I can tell you this," she told Riley, one of her coworkers who came in to remove her empty tray. "When I get back to work, I'll have a new respect for the injured."

Riley had laughed. "I know what you mean. I broke my leg once and had to be holed up for three days at the hospital in Dallas." She shook her head. "I guess it's true what they say, that medical personnel makes the worst patients."

"I've been tolerable, though?" Missy asked, causing Riley to chuckle.

"You're the easiest patient I've had all year." She looked towards the door. "Now if room two would be as good."

The clinic had only four overnight rooms for such occasions and she had been waiting on room two. Mr. Dillard, an older gentleman, was a contractor for hire who'd had a large tree branch fall on him a few days back. He had a broken foot, but because of his age, Dr. Conner wanted to watch him for a while. Mr. Dillard wasn't too pleased about the stay and was very vocal in his complaints.

Over the next few hours, many friends visited Melissa in the room. She convinced Reece to stick around, but he had to step outside for a few phone calls.

He seemed distracted and when he stepped back into the room after the fifth call, she realized why.

"Oh, your horse was supposed to come today." She frowned.

"It did. He's there and safe and sound in the barn."

"Reece, you don't have to stay." She felt guilty for keeping him from his work and commitment. "I'm out of hot water now," she said, sitting up slowly.

He shook his head. "Are you kicking me out?" he asked with a smile.

"No, of course not. But, if you need to—"

"Missy, I'm where I want to be." He took her hand.

"But if you need to—"

He stopped her by leaning down and placing a kiss on her lips. She closed her eyes and enjoyed the feeling of him.

She did convince him around dinnertime to go down the street and grab a proper meal at Mama's since the clinic didn't serve very good food. She was happily surprised when he brought back a large box of food for her. She ate every bite, knowing that the return of her appetite meant she was on the mend.

A few hours later, she once again tried to convince Reece to go home and get a good night's sleep, but he wouldn't hear it. Instead, he propped his legs on the edge of her bed and leaned back in the chair and closed his eyes.

She watched him for a while but must have drifted off. She woke when the night nurse, Stephanie, came in to check on her and take her vitals. He woke and peppered Stephanie with questions. She couldn't help feeling more in love with him every moment he stood by her side.

That next day she was released, and Reece talked her into going back to his place instead of her own so he could watch her closely. They stopped by her house and grabbed a few of her clothes and things so she could stay with him. She was told by Dr. Conner not to come back to work for a whole week. Reece quickly replied that he would make sure she rested the whole time.

When they drove up to his place, she was surprised to see all of her family and friends on the front porch of Reece's home.

"What's going on?" She looked over at him in question.

"Just a small get-together." He smiled at her. "I thought

it would be nice to have your family celebrate your recovery."

She smiled. "Sounds great. God, I hope my mom baked a pie." She heard her stomach growl and laughed when his did as well.

"Me too," he said before rushing around and helping her out of the truck.

That evening, after everyone had finally left the house, he sat on the sofa with Missy and watched the rest of the baseball game on the big screen while she slept. Her head was in his lap, and he gently stroked her hair. She had to wear a large white collar around her neck to keep it steady, and he noticed that she moved very slowly because of her ribs.

She had stitches in her head and shoulder that needed to stay dry and clean, which meant she'd have to be careful bathing. She had a bottle of pain pills that she had to take twice a day with food. She'd downed her first pill after eating some of her mother's home cooking and pie. The pills made her drowsy and she'd lay down on the sofa and quickly fallen asleep. Everyone had cleaned up quietly and left.

He looked down at her in his lap and felt his heart skip. He'd never imagined caring for someone as much as he cared for her. He'd meant it when he'd told her he was more than just in love with her. He'd never felt this way about anyone in his entire life, even Ryan. It went beyond anything he'd ever known could exist, and he knew what he wanted to do about it. He just wanted to make sure she was healthy again before he took the next step.

She stirred and opened her eyes, but he saw that they were still cloudy. "Want to move into the bedroom?" He brushed her hair away from her face.

"I'd kill for a hot shower." She stretched her arms straight in front of her and moaned a little with some pain.

He frowned.

"I can take a bath." He helped her sit up. "As long as I make sure to keep my head and shoulder dry."

He nodded and stood up. "I'll go start the water."

"Reece?"

"Make it hot. My muscles are sore." She stretched her legs straight out in front of her.

He nodded and left the room. When he got into the bathroom, he started the water in the tub then looked at himself in the mirror.

He needed a plan. He wanted to make it special for her. She deserved special. He closed his eyes and felt like banging his head against the mirror. Then an idea came to him.

Holly. Holly would know what Missy had always dreamed about. He'd have to make sure to stop by the bookstore tomorrow and talk to her and see if she could help him out.

He walked over and dumped some of the soap she'd left in the shower into the bath water, causing it to bubble up. He tested the temperature and made sure it was hot but not boiling. Then he walked into the next room to help her in.

It took some doing, but finally, she leaned back into the water and sighed.

"I never thought undressing you would be such a challenge." He chuckled and sat on the edge of the tub.

"I never thought that once you undressed me, I'd think about anything other than being with you." She smiled and then sighed and leaned her head back. "But getting out of that neck brace feels so good."

"Don't overdo it," he warned, concerned she was moving her neck too much.

"I'm fine." She looked up at him. "Really."

He nodded. "I'll let you enjoy your bath. When you're ready to get out, call for me. I don't want to chance you slipping."

She nodded slightly. "Can you dim the lights?"

He walked over and flipped on the light in the hall and turned off the bathroom light. "Is this okay?"

"Yes, much better." She rested back. "I may just stay in here all night. Too bad you don't have a tub with jets."

"For you, I'll add it to the list." When he walked out to the kitchen, he did just that. They had a running list of things that needed to be fixed or replaced.

He looked at the three pages stuck to the front of the fridge and added Jacuzzi tub under the master bathroom heading.

He looked around and the images his mind had created earlier about the three kids running around returned; he let them come. He walked around the house and added items to the list that would make his dreams a reality.

When he was done, he could picture the life he and Missy would share. Now all he had to do was ask the hardest question any man ever had to ask.

CHAPTER 16

*M*issy was going crazy. It was hard enough to be hurting physically, but she was also bored out of her mind.

Most days during her week-long quarantine, as she called it, she spent lying on the sofa. Five days after being released, she was feeling better and would secretly take off her neck brace whenever Reece was out of the house.

She had ventured on several occasions to the front porch, so she could watch him breaking the horses. The Corals were within sight of the front deck and she enjoyed watching him work with the horses. He had gotten on the back of a black stallion yesterday, and her nerves had almost had her jumping out of her skin.

She couldn't stand seeing him fly through the air, even if he was laughing like he was having the most fun of his life. She actually started biting her fingernails, something she'd never done before.

How would she ever get used to seeing him do this for a living? Would she always worry this much about him?

She leaned against the porch railing and watched him now. He really did look like he enjoyed being tossed around. She knew that he had aches and pains from the jolting, but for the most part, he didn't complain.

She frowned. Actually, he never complained. It was something about him that she found utterly fascinating. Being a nurse, she knew that most tough men turned into big babies the moment they got a sliver, but not Reece.

She thought of how she'd acted since her car accident and sighed. She'd done enough complaining for the both of them.

Her ribs were feeling better and she was set to get the stitches out the day before she returned to work. She was only getting headaches when there was a bright light or loud noise. Her neck was starting to feel better, and she was ready to ditch the collar.

She reached up and touched it, wishing she could remove it now. But she was within eyesight of Reece and knew he would stop what he was doing and make her put it back on. She smiled. He was wonderful at taking care of her.

He'd cooked every meal since her she'd come to stay with him. She would sit on a bar stool and watch him move around the kitchen. She sighed now, watching how his shirt stuck to him. Summer was in full swing and even standing out on the front porch for ten minutes usually soaked her shirt with sweat. His was stuck to him and she was enjoying every line that was exposed.

She saw sweat dripping down his face and arms as he patiently worked with the horse. He was wonderful with the animals. She knew that some busters used force and anger to get the animals to do what they wanted. Not

Reece. He spoke to the animal softly, patiently, and praised it when it did what he asked. He rubbed it on the neck and gave it treats of sugar cubes or apple slices when he was done teaching it something.

She could imagine him being the same way around kids. He was wonderful with her nephews; she'd seen it firsthand. She walked back into the cool house and imagined raising a family with him here.

She looked around and smiled. This was a great place for kids. Their kids. She leaned against the bar and thought about how to get him to see what she was seeing. She'd never thought about getting married or having kids with anyone before; no one else would have done.

Picking up her cell phone, she called Holly.

"Hey, how are you doing?" Holly asked.

"I'm good." She undid her collar and moved her neck to test the waters. It was a little sore, but not as bad as it used to be. "I have a question."

"Shoot."

"Do you know how to propose to a man?"

"What? What?" Holly asked, her voice getting a little louder.

She laughed. "I want to marry Reece, but I'm not sure how to go about asking him."

Holly was silent for a while. "I'm not sure. I've never asked someone to marry me before."

"I know that." She chuckled. "Haven't you read a book or something?"

It was quiet for a while. "It's customary for the man—"

"Holly, I don't know if Reece has thought of asking me. Besides, I don't want to wait. I know what I want, and I don't want to wait around for it."

Her friend laughed. "Tell you what, how about I think about it for a while and give you a call back later tonight."

"Okay." She frowned. Then she heard the bell chime above the bookstore door and realized she'd interrupted her friend's workday. It was really hard taking a whole week off of work and remembering that everyone else had to be at work. "I'm sorry to interrupt your day."

"It's not a big deal. I'm just getting ready for reading time. I'll give you a call back later tonight."

"Okay, thanks." She hung up and rested her head in her hands.

An idea started to form in her mind and she jumped up from the stool. It would take some planning, but she knew there was no reward without a little hard work.

Reece looked down at his phone and frowned. He didn't know what Holly's text message meant, but he trusted her enough to alter his plans. He texted her back and told her it was a go for that evening and to put his plan into motion. He just prayed that Holly would be able to pull it off in time.

Looking at the clock on his phone, he frowned and realized he'd have to cut his workday short by a few hours. When he walked into the house, he heard Melissa back in the shower and stripped his clothes off as he walked into the room.

"Hi," he said before opening the shower door.

"Oh," she turned and jumped a little. "Hi." She smiled. "I didn't know you were done already."

"I clocked off early tonight. What do you say to dinner in town?"

She smiled. "Sounds great." She wrapped her arms around his neck, rubbing her wet body against his, and he knew that they would be late to their own engagement.

When they finally drove into town, only ten minutes late, they parked in front of Mama's and he turned to her. She was wearing a flowing summer dresses that showed off her shoulders. She'd replaced the big white bandages on her shoulder and forehead with skin-colored ones.

He wore a pair of his best jeans and one of his best button-up shirts and boots. They looked the part and he felt his nerves kicking in as he helped her out of the car.

"Would you mind?" He stopped her from walking towards Mama's. "Holly had a copy of her book for me. I promised I'd swing by and grab it next time I was in town." He nodded to the bookstore next door.

"Sure," she smiled. "I was supposed to talk to her about something." He saw a sparkle in her eye.

They walked next door, hand in hand, and he opened the door for her, excited about what was coming next.

It was dark in the bookstore, and Melissa wondered if her friend had closed up shop early that day. She glanced down at her watch and frowned. The bookstore should still be open for at least another hour.

"Holly?" she called out.

"She's not here," Reece said behind her. He took her hand and walked with her towards the back fireplace. There in front of the fireplace was a small table set for two. Candles lit the table, and white lights were strung around the bookshelves, giving the whole room a low glow. There were plates full of wonderful-smelling food on the table and a bottle of wine with two glasses. A bundle of red roses sat in the middle of the table that was covered with a cream-colored tablecloth.

"What?" She stopped walking and turned towards Reece, who just smiled down at her.

"I thought it would be nice to have dinner by ourselves instead of a crowded diner." He nodded to the plates. "They might be a little cold since our shower ran a little long." He chuckled and pulled her closer.

"You?" She swallowed. "You put this all together?"

He nodded and took her hand and walked her to the table where he pulled out the chair for her.

"Hang on," she said, pulling off her collar and setting it aside. "There." She moved her neck around. "Just for tonight," she said when he started to object. He looked at her and then finally nodded.

"Just for tonight." He held the chair for her and she walked over and sat down. He poured her a glass of wine then sat down.

"This is wonderful. I can't believe Holly didn't spill about your plans when I talked to her a while ago."

He chuckled. "She can be bribed into keeping a secret."

"Oh?" She looked up at him. "You'll have to tell me all your secrets." She smiled.

The food was still warm and delicious and when they

were both done eating, he walked over and took a large cake from behind Holly's counter. It was covered and when he sat it in front of her, he looked nervous.

"I—I had Holly make this cake special." He removed the cover and then set it down on the table.

She looked down at the cake and her smile fell away from her face. There, in white icing and red iced roses were the words, *"Missy, will you marry me?"*

She turned to Reece, who was now on his knee next to her, a slick black box in his hand. A beautiful diamond ring sat in it. He reached for her hand and cleared his throat.

"Missy, you're the woman of my dreams." He shook his head. "Actually, my dreams have never been this good." He smiled at her. "I can't imagine a moment without you by my side. I want to be with you every second of the day. Every night I want to reach over and feel your heart beat along with mine. Please say that you'll marry me?"

She swallowed and looked around. The small bookstore had been turned into something out of a fairytale she'd dreamed up in her youth. This was the moment she'd dreamed of her entire life. Looking over, she noticed that Reece was looking at her, waiting. Nodding her head, she swallowed and smiled.

"Yes." It came out as a squeak. "Of course, I'll marry you." She laughed as he leaned up and took her into his arms and hugged her gently.

When she pulled back, she looked up into his green eyes. "You're the man of my dreams. I knew it the moment you opened your eyes on my examining table." She smiled. "I want to make a life with you."

He pulled her close and slipped the ring on her finger.

It fit perfectly, and she couldn't help but smile when she saw it sparkle in the soft light.

"It's perfect." She looked up at him. "You're perfect." She reached over and kissed him again. "I couldn't have asked for a more perfect moment."

*R*eece stood in his corral and looked off towards the house. Melissa would be home from work any minute. He still had a shock of joy run through him when he thought of this house as theirs. She'd moved her stuff in two weeks earlier, and they had told their families about the engagement.

His business was taking off, and he had a string of jobs waiting for him. He'd had to start taking bookings since he was losing track of all the jobs.

Missy had helped him organize his books and schedule. They had set up a small office for him in one of the bedrooms and had talked about getting him a laptop so he could do all his scheduling online.

He turned and watched her drive up in her new car, a four-door this time. He liked that it was a bigger car but wished she'd gone with a truck. She'd stuck to the smaller one for better gas mileage.

He waved to her and tied the horse he'd been working

with to the fence. He hopped the fence and placed a kiss on her lips. "How was your day?"

She smiled up at him. "Good." Then she frowned. "I heard from my friend in Houston."

"Hmm?" He brushed her hair away from her face gently. He would never tire of touching it, of seeing her eyes melt when he did.

"About seeing your brother."

He stilled then nodded.

"She told me that the police had showed up less than an hour after they'd moved man who had been shot to a private room, and they'd removed him."

"What does that mean?"

She shrugged. "It could mean a couple things."

He dropped his arms and took a few paces away from her.

"Did you get his name?"

She shook her head. "He hadn't provided one. We had him down as John Doe. But I was right about the date and description. Some of us put our notes about noticeable details. Several of the nurses had written green eyes, brown hair, and a small scar above his left eye."

He stopped pacing and turned to her. "Left eye?" She nodded, and he felt his stomach turn. "Ryan."

"Are you sure?"

"Yeah." He closed his eyes and remembered his brother's face. "I gave it to him."

"Well, Carol—that's the head nurse that works in Houston—she says that it was noted that the police came and took him away. They claimed he was dangerous." She looked down at her hands, and he felt his world spin. His brother, his twin had turned out worse than their old man. No! He wouldn't believe it until he saw it for himself.

"I think it's time I hired someone to find him. I won't believe it until I see it for myself."

She smiled and nodded. "I was hoping you'd say that." She pulled out a piece of paper from her purse. "Here."

"What is it?" He looked down at it and frowned.

"It's a receipt for hiring a private detective." She smiled. "I talked to my father and he highly recommends this man. I guess he represented him a long time ago." She waved her arm. "Anyway, dad swears he's the best."

"You hired a detective to find my brother?" When she nodded, he pulled her closer to him and kissed her. "You are the best."

She smiled up at him. "I know."

He laughed.

PROLOGUE

Holly was going mad. It had been two weeks since she'd shut down the old bookstore and moved. Two weeks of living in a strange place, in someone else's apartment. Two weeks of the daily stress of coordinating and working with all the contractors and laborers. Two weeks without work. But, other than a sore back from sleeping in a strange bed, she was loving every minute of it.

She couldn't stop herself from rushing down to the old brick building she'd known her entire life and seeing the work that was being done on it. Sure, currently it didn't look much different than when the tornado had ripped through town over two years ago. But, if you looked closely, you could see a method to the madness.

There were two large dumpsters in the back alley behind what was going to be her new business. On several occasions, they had been full to the top and hauled away, replaced by two new empty ones.

As she stood in the middle of the building her mother

and her had worked all their lives in, she couldn't help but smile. It was an early Sunday morning in late fall and she knew the place would be quiet. She loved coming here when the workers weren't banging around, making messing. She could actually see the vision she and Mr. Nolan had designed.

Who would have known that the old mayor had an architecture background? Not her, but when she finally built up enough nerve to ask him about updating his building, he'd not only jumped on board but had fronted the entire cost himself. Sure, the building was his and he could do whatever he wanted with it, but she never expected him to include her tiny apartment upstairs in all the plans.

"Why not redo the whole place?" He'd said, walking around the downstairs. "In the last two years, there's been more repair on your apartment than down here. If we're going in for a penny, why not a pound and do it all."

She'd jumped at the chance, of course. He'd been right; her apartment was in dire need. The roof leaked during heavy storms and some of the old wooden floorboards had come up. She'd covered them with rugs, but still, she tended to stub her toes on them if she wasn't careful. All of the plumbing and electric for the entire building was in dire need. She lost electricity more often due to not enough volts going through the breaker box.

So, Mr. Nolan and she had marched down to the bank and signed an agreement that the town's lawyer, Grant Holton had written up. The next week she started receiving bids on the construction and moved everything out, including herself. At least until everything was completed and according to the latest news from her contractor wouldn't be until sometime early spring.

She looked around and smiled. She didn't mind all the mess and hassles her life was in right now, especially since she knew what it would look like afterward. Her furniture and the bookstore's inventory were in storage, tucked away until next spring when she could open Holly's. The first bookstore slash coffeehouse slash wine bar to grace the small town of Fairplay Texas.

"Dreaming of what it will look like when it's done?" She heard behind her, causing her to jump a little.

"Oh," she rested her hand over her heart. "Mr. Nolan, I didn't expect you."

The older gentlemen stood in the doorway, his hands tucked into his pants, looking tired. She'd known Roy Nolan all of her life, he'd been the town's mayor for as long as anyone could remember, that was until his wife of thirty plus years had gone plain nuts. Then he'd quietly stepped down as mayor and retreated into his large white home just a few blocks from there. His only child, Travis had left town the same night they had hauled his mother away to the state penitentiary. No one in town had heard from him since. All though it was rumored that Savannah Douglas has visited him on several occasions in the past few months.

"It looks a mess now. Doesn't it girlie?" He said, using her nickname for her as he walked into the empty room. All the walls were gone, and the hardwood floor was completely ripped up, leaving only cement.

"I can still see the potential." She turned and looked at him. "Especially with all the wonderful drawings you did." She smiled.

He nodded. "Well, girlie, you had a wonderful idea for this place. I had big dreams for this town." He sighed and looked out the large front windows towards Main Street.

She walked over and rested her hand on his arm. "This is a wonderful first step."

He nodded. "I had hoped that…" He started and then shook his head.

"What?" She waited.

"I had hoped that Travis would come back. He loved this town. Everything I've worked so hard for…" He paused again, and Holly felt his arm stiffen. "Everything I did was for that boy."

She started to worry when he began shaking.

"Mr. Nolan? Are you alright?" She gripped his arm tighter, but he seemed to just look off into the distance.

When he hunched forward and started to fall, she gripped tighter, trying to hold him upright, but the man's massive frame was no match for her tiny five-four. He hit the floor hard, causing her to land on her knees.

When she looked over, she saw that his face had gone completely white. Rushing up to him, she rolled him over onto his back and listened for a heartbeat. When she couldn't find one, she rushed over to where she'd set her purse down and pulled out her cell phone and dialed 911 as she knelt beside him again.

"Hang on Mr. Nolan, help is on the way." She reassured him, holding his hand in hers as a tear slipped down her face.

BREAKING TRAVIS

CHAPTER 1

*T*ravis stood in front of his old house and hated being there. It was too dark to see anything clearly, especially since all the lights in the massive place were out. Too many memories flooded his mind. He wanted to escape them, but he knew he couldn't, not until all his business was done and he could start fresh.

It had been almost a month since he'd gotten word that his father had passed away from a massive heart attack. It had taken his father's lawyer almost two weeks to track him down in Montana. The fact that the man was his ex-fiancée Alexis' husband had just been the icing on the bitter cake he'd been eating for the last four years.

He grabbed his duffel bag from the rental car and started walking towards the house. But instead of heading to the big house, he circled around the back and climbed the stars to his old apartment above the garage. It was just past midnight and his flight had been delayed due to a thunderstorm in Colorado. He was exhausted.

Dropping his bag inside the door, he took a few steps

into the apartment and knew instantly that he wasn't alone. Every muscle in his body tensed as he scanned the dark room. In the last two years, there had been plenty of fights and as he prepared his body for the blows, his mind refused to hear the signal his nose was sending to him.

The first blow skimmed his jaw, sending him back a few steps. When he reached out with his fist, he thought he'd connect with something. Instead, he hit only air. The next blow took him by surprise in his gut, forcing him to reach out and grab what he could of his attacker.

When he grabbed a hold of clothes, he stepped back to flip his assailant over, but tripped on his duffel bag and ended up on the ground. He'd taken his assaulter down with him, so he rolled a few times until he ended up on top.

"What are you doing in my house?" He demanded at the same time a fist came up and connected with his left eye. He moaned with pain just as the body underneath him stilled.

"Your house?"

It was a woman's voice, causing him to momentarily drop his guard.

She shoved his shoulder and leg hard until he fell off her. He landed on the floor holding his throbbing left eye.

Then the lights flipped on and thereby the door to his apartment stood a warrior. Her long red hair flowed down past her breasts, which were covered nicely with a teal tank top and matching shorts.

"Travis?" She stood looking down at him.

He dropped his hand away from his face and looked at her with watery eyes. "Do I know you?"

She shook her head and put her hands on her hips.

"Holly Bridles." He just looked at her. "I run the bookstore."

"Sure, you do." He said getting up off the ground. "That doesn't explain what you're doing in my house?"

She sighed. "I live here." She looked around the apartment and for the first time, he realized it was clean. Clean, cleaned. Everything of his was gone, except the furniture, his parents had bought him when he'd moved out of the big house.

He groaned. "That's just great." He turned and looked at her again.

She was still standing by the front door and he wondered why his father would have rented the place out to a librarian.

"I guess I didn't know he rented the place out."

"He didn't." She said quickly. His eyebrows shot up. "I'm not renting the place."

Well, that cleared it up, he thought. It was bound to happen after all the ink on his parents' divorce had been dry for almost three years now. His father was bound to have moved on. He looked at the woman's skimpy outfit and smiled a little. Way to go, dad, he thought. Then he frowned as she stepped further into the light. What was a man in his late sixties doing with someone so young?

"I didn't know you were going to be back." She crossed her arms over her chest, no doubt because he'd been staring at those lovely tits of hers.

He blinked and stepped closer. Her hands dropped and rested by her sides in fists and he wondered how such a small package could pack such a big punch.

"I guess I'll head over to the big house until we sort this all out." He bent to pick up his duffel bag. When he stood back up, he noticed her biting her bottom lip with worry. He turned and walked out of his apartment without another word.

Okay, he told himself on the short walk towards the back door of the big house, new list. As he opened the back door of the massive house, he listed them off in his mind. Get rid of dad's hussy, which was really too bad since he could have used the detraction while he was in town, sell the house, and get the hell out of Fairplay Texas.

Holly stood in her doorway and bit her bottom lip. Travis was back. What did that mean? Was he going to kick her out of the apartment? Without the store being opened, she doubted she could afford renting another place. At least until the doors opened.

The reading of Mr. Nolan's will had been postponed until Travis made it back into town. Until then, it had been agreed that the construction would continue. Shutting the door, she leaned up against the cool wood and rested her head back, closing her eyes. She was in deep trouble. What if there wasn't anything about their agreement in his will? Would Travis hold up his father's wishes? Would she be kicked to the curb? What about her shop? Would construction stop?

Shaking her head clear of the million questions running through it, she walked back towards the bedroom, she grabbed the water bottle she'd been getting which had caused her to hear the front door open earlier. She stopped and looked back at the door. Yup, it was locked and bolted. Something she did every night, which meant, he had a key to the place. She walked towards the door and snapped on the chain for good measure.

Travis was trouble. Had been most of his life and probably would be until the day he died. Too bad, she thought crawling into bed. The man had a body like the Gods and a face to melt even the hardest hearts. She sighed and closed her eyes, burying her face into the pillow. What she wouldn't give to feel a good man on top of her like he'd been a short while ago. Giggling to herself, she decided she had gone too long without a date.

Then she frowned when she remembered she lived in a small town and there were no good men to date. Closing her eyes tighter, she tried to get the feeling of being that close to a man out of her mind.

She woke early that next morning and headed into check on construction. Since Mr. Nolan's death, she spent most of her time making sure everything was on track. Helping with ordering and organizing the materials, coordinating the construction crews. Solving any issues or questions they had during the entire process. Some of the men had even gotten her, her own hardhat and tool belt.

Not to mention that if she got out of the apartment, it would be harder for Travis to track her down and kick her to the curb. Since she was working on only a few hours of sleep, she was having a hard time concentrating. She stood off to the side and watched the men work and just couldn't muster up what the place would look like once it was finished.

The day didn't get any better when an hour past lunch, a water pipe broke in the apartment and started leaking downstairs. It took every man on sight to finally clear the standing water on the cement floor, so the workers could continue hanging the drywall. Thankfully the damage had been left to just a small spot that was already being patched.

She stood in what would be her new storeroom looking up at the work the drywaller had done when she felt a tap on her shoulder. She turned expecting to see a work but was shocked when Travis stood there looking down at her with a frown and a very black and swollen left eye.

"What's all this?" He demanded.

Her eyebrows shot up in question. He had his hands on his hips and a very impatient look on his face. He was wearing a dress shirt and dress pants. Even his shoes were shiny and new looking. His hair had been combed back and he'd shaved since she'd seen him last night. "You shouldn't be in here without a hard hat." She walked over to the back doorway and grabbed a yellow hat and handed it over to him.

He set it on his head and demanded in a louder voice, which rose above all the pounding and sawing. "What is this?" He motioned around him.

"This is my store." She frowned. "Remember?"

"Your bookstore?"

She nodded. "Yes."

He took a deep breath and rubbed his forehead. "What I mean is why is it under construction.

She frowned. "Because the wiring in the building was shot, there was still roofing damage from the tornado, and…"

"I mean…" He ground out, interrupting her. "Why is my father paying for this all?" He yelled, over the new loud noises coming from a few feet away and waved a stack of bills at her. She was used to the noises by now; after all, she'd been on site every day for the last month.

"Because it's his building." She yelled back and looked at him like he was crazy.

He grabbed her arm and marched her out the back door. Here there were other men using table saws and nail guns. He stopped and looked around, then continued to walk her towards the little garden area she had. She'd been raising tomatoes and squash and even had a little picnic table and swing along the tall fence.

"Why is my father paying a lot of money to have you rebuild your store?" He finally said, dropping her arm and waiving the bills again.

"Because it's his building and he had a vision." She crossed her arms over her chest.

"Great," He said, rolling his eyes. "Now he was having visions."

She frowned. "Your father wanted to rebuild the bookstore."

"I'm sure he did." He looked her over. She had put on her standard work clothes, old jeans, button up blouse, and an old pair of boots. She'd tied her hair up in two braids, which lay across her shoulders out of her way.

"What does that mean?" She asked, putting her hands on her hips.

He laughed, "Listen, you're very attractive and I'm sure you had your usefulness when my father was alive, but there's just no way I'm going to continue all this." He motioned towards the building.

She stood there shocked. He was going to take it all away from her.

"I don't know what kind of… arrangement you and my

father had, but he's gone now, and you can expect that anything he was giving you won't be coming from me." He turned to go.

"I'm sorry?" She said to his back.

He turned and looked at her, then sighed and turned back to her. "If I was sticking around town, maybe I'd help you out, but I'm not. I'm heading over to the lawyers right now and putting all this"—he motioned to the building—"on the market. So, if I were you, I'd pack up what you can and get going because if you're still on my property by tonight, I'll call the cops."

She lost the last thread of her temper at that moment. "How dare you." She took a step closer to him. "Your father was a great man. A man with a vision for this town and in one day you plan to wipe everything he worked hard for out."

He took a step closer to her. "You'll want to be careful what you say to me." His eyes bore into hers.

She took another step closer to him until they were almost nose-to-nose. Well, they would have been if he wasn't a foot taller than her. She blinked back her anger before finally speaking.

"You're heading over to Grant's now?" She asked, throwing him off balance.

Grant normally worked out of his house, but since there were now two kids, a three-year-old and a two-month-old around, he tended to be in the office more and more. He claimed it was hard to take a business call when kids were screaming in the background. But everyone in town knew the real reason, Alex, his wife, kicked him out so he would actually get some work done instead of playing with the kids all the time.

When he finally nodded, she said. "Good, I'll just walk over there with you." She turned and started walking down the street.

He laughed and followed her. "Why? Do you really think that my father would have left you anything?"

"No, I know he didn't." She glanced over her shoulder at him.

"Then why tag along?" He kept in step with her easily, noticing that she marched a little faster.

"Because I know what he wanted, and I can only hope that he had the brains to put it all down on paper before he left us." She said, a little breathless.

By the time they walked into Grant Holton's office, she was completely out of breath. Her face was red from the heat and some of her hair had come loose from the braids.

When she marched back towards his office, Travis followed. Knocking on the door quickly, she stepped in without waiting for an answer. Grant was on the phone and when he saw her, he nodded, but when he saw Travis, he apologized and quickly hung up the phone.

"Travis?" He stood and held out his hand. "It's good to have you back in town."

Travis was completely floored. Here was the man who had in every sense taken his future bride away from him. Then Travis' mother had shot and tried to kill him! Now, he stood in his office and the man was actually being nice like none of that had ever happened.

"Grant." He shook his hand and stood there like he didn't know what to say next.

There were pictures of Alex and Grant's kids and animals all over the office, Travis glanced at a few, but then turned his eyes towards the floor. It was too hard to see Alex in those pictures, happily holding the chubby babies.

"Travis and I would like to know what's in his father's will," Holly said, crossing her arms over her chest.

"Now Holly, we've been through this a dozen times. I can't tell you what's in Mr. Nolan's will unless Travis here," he nodded towards him. "Says it's okay."

She glared at him until finally, he nodded. "I'll allow it, I suppose." What harm could it be? After all, there was no way his father would have left anything for this woman.

"Fine, if you'll take a seat I'll just pull it up." Grant sat back behind his desk. "Did you just get into town?" He asked.

Travis shook his head. "Last night." He said, looking down at his fingernails, not wanting to make eye contact with the man his mother had almost killed.

"Good, I hope your trip was good. We're really sorry about your dad, he was a good man."

Travis glanced up at Grant quickly. "Thanks." He said, looking back down at his fingers.

"Here it is," Grant said, getting both of their attention. "I'll cut to the chase," he looked up at them. "What it says in here is that the house and all the assets go to you Travis."

Travis nodded then smiled and glanced over at Holly.

"With explicit orders that any projects currently underway continue with you overseeing them or you'd forfeit everything else."

"What?" He said, sitting forward. "What does that mean?"

"Well, your father started a few projects over the last few months. As I can see, you already know about the bookstore, he also started renovation work on the old theater and on the building a new park just outside of town."

"I don't understand." He stood up.

"Earlier this year, your father talked to me about wanting to put some of his money back into the town. He started a few smaller projects at first, putting a fresh coat of paint on the town hall, putting in a few park benches, some new streetlights. Then Holly approached him about updating the bookstore and her apartment. I guess that started him thinking about some of the other projects he'd been putting off."

"Can they just continue without me?"

Grant shook his head. "Your father put it in his will that if you didn't oversee them all, they would stop completely."

"Good, then stop them, I don't care." He turned to go.

"If they stop, you'll be left with nothing. Everything your father owned will go to the town, to finish the projects without you." Grant said.

Travis stopped, his hand on the doorknob, he needed his inheritance if he was going to get out of the world he'd been in the last three years. He was getting tired and wanted to do something more with his life. He spun around and glared at the woman he thought was the cause of his father's crazy scheme. "This was all your doing."

Holly stood up and glared right back at him. "Don't be silly."

"Travis, Holly had nothing to do with this. There's a note here," he held out a sealed envelope. "from your father."

"You mean; I'm stuck in this town until all of his little projects are done?"

Grant handed him the note. "If you want your inheritance, you are. There is one more thing in here." Grant looked down at Holly. "Holly stays in the apartment, rent free until the building is done. Once the building is completed, there are more instructions that I'm not at liberty to discuss until such time."

Travis walked out of the building without another word. He stood on the sidewalk and ripped open his father's note.

Son,

I know how hard the last few years have been on you. I wanted you to know that I'm proud of you. I've checked up on you and know that you've cleaned up your life. I couldn't be prouder of you.

I'm asking you for a favor now. If you're reading this, it means that I have left some unfinished business in town. These people deserve our thanks. They have been there for us in our time of need. You may not have seen it, but each and every person in this town is behind you.

I'll ask this last thing for you. Please finish what I have started so the town and the wonderful people in it can heal.

I love you son

He was trapped. No matter what he did, he had a sinking feeling that there was no way he would ever leave Fairplay again.

This is a work of fiction. Names, characters, places, and incidents are either the product of the author's imagination or are used fictitiously, and any resemblance to actual persons, living or dead, business establishments, events, or locales is entirely coincidental.

MISSY'S MOMENT

DIGITAL ISBN: 978-1-942896-50-0

PRINT ISBN: 978-1-942896-51-7

Copyright © 2014 Jill Sanders

All rights reserved.

Copyeditor: Erica Ellis – inkdeepediting.com

The Pride Series

Finding Pride

Discovering Pride

Returning Pride

Lasting Pride

Serving Pride

Red Hot Christmas

My Sweet Valentine

Return To Me

Rescue Me

The Secret Series

Secret Seduction

Secret Pleasure

Secret Guardian

Secret Passions

Secret Identity

Secret Sauce

The West Series

Loving Lauren

Taming Alex

Holding Haley

Missy's Moment

Breaking Travis

Roping Ryan

Wild Bride

Corey's Catch

Tessa's Turn

The Grayton Series

Last Resort

Someday Beach

Rip Current

In Too Deep

Swept Away

High Tide

Lucky Series

Unlucky In Love

Sweet Resolve

Best of Luck

A Little Luck

Silver Cove Series

Silver Lining

French Kiss

Happy Accident

Hidden Charm

A Silver Cove Christmas

Entangled Series – Paranormal Romance

The Awakening

The Beckoning

The Ascension

Haven, Montana Series

Closer to You

Never Let Go

Holding On

Pride Oregon Series

A Dash of Love

My Kind of Love

Season of Love

Tis the Season

Dare to Love

Where I Belong

Wildflowers Series

Summer Nights

Summer Heat

Stand Alone Books

Twisted Rock

For a complete list of books:

http://JillSanders.com

ABOUT THE AUTHOR

Jill Sanders is a New York Times, USA Today, and international bestselling author of Sweet Contemporary Romance, Romantic Suspense, Western Romance, and Paranormal Romance novels. With over 55 books in eleven series, translations into several different languages, and audiobooks there's plenty to choose from. Look for Jill's bestselling stories wherever romance books are sold or visit her at jillsanders.com

Jill comes from a large family with six siblings, including an identical twin. She was raised in the Pacific Northwest and later relocated to Colorado for college and a successful IT career before discovering her talent for writing sweet and sexy page-turners. After Colorado, she decided to move south, living in Texas and now making her home along the Emerald Coast of Florida. You will find that the settings of several of her series are inspired by her time spent living in these areas. She has two sons and off-set the testosterone in her house by adopting three furry little ladies that provide her company while she's locked in her writing cave. She enjoys heading to the beach, hiking, swimming, wine-tasting, and pickleball with her husband, and of course writing. If you have read any of her books, you may also notice that there is a love of food, especially sweets! She has been blamed for a few added pounds by her assistant, editor, and fans... donuts or pie anyone?

facebook.com/JillSandersBooks

twitter.com/JillMSanders

bookbub.com/authors/jill-sanders

9 781942 896517